LAST CHANCE FIRST

I was trapped on a world where creatures hadn't evolved. They'd been made up, assembled—and they had once been human!

Suddenly the pistol stopped firing. I watched in horrible fascination as the plastic seemed to corrode before my eyes. On impulse I squeezed and the thing crushed into bits.

Mad and scared, I took out the portapack and told the computer to take off. The portapack began to corrode. Within seconds it was useless.

And then the suit felt funny; it became hard to breathe. I screamed in sheer fury, rushed to the web-wall separating me from my world, and banged my fist against the charred spot I'd made. As I did, my gloves crumbled, yet I pounded still in utter helplessness.

Nobody had ever beaten Bar Holliday before —but there was a first time for everything!

Also by Jack L. Chalker
Published by Ballantine Books:

AND THE DEVIL WILL DRAG YOU UNDER

A JUNGLE OF STARS

THE SAGA OF THE WELL WORLD
Volume 1: *Midnight at the Well of Souls*
Volume 2: *Exiles at the Well of Souls*
Volume 3: *Quest for the Well of Souls*
Volume 4: *The Return of Nathan Brazil*
Volume 5: *Twilight at the Well of Souls:*
             The Legacy of Nathan Brazil

THE FOUR LORDS OF THE DIAMOND
Book One: *Lilith: A Snake in the Grass*
Book Two: *Cerberus: A Wolf in the Fold*

THE WEB
OF THE
CHOZEN

Jack L. Chalker

A Del Rey Book

BALLANTINE BOOKS • NEW YORK

A Del Rey Book
Published by Ballantine Books

Copyright © 1978 by Jack L. Chalker

Library of Congress Catalog Card Number: 77-25227

ISBN 0-345-30455-1

Manufactured in the United States of America

First Edition: February 1978
Second Printing: May 1982

Cover art by Ralph McQuarrie

To the immortal spirit of the Tasmanian Liberation Army: Jake Waldman, Joan Serrano, Stu Tait, and Ned Brooks, good Canadian botanists all, and for Bob Tucker, who singlehandedly conquers continents.

There is an apocryphal story about the time when Mark Twain visited England and was introduced to George Bernard Shaw. Shaw was unsure about the folksy man of letters, but figured that anyone who sold as many books as Twain did must be intelligent, and invited the American to a meeting of the Fabian Society. Twain listened to the speeches, mostly dull, about what sort of utopia these people dreamed of for masses considerably lower on the socioeconomic ladder than themselves. Finally, they asked for questions.

"This utopia you talk about," Twain is alleged to have muttered, "what's it supposed to do?"

He was informed that in this wonderful world of the future all men would share in the world's wealth, that no human being would ever want for food, clothing or shelter.

Twain was reportedly thoughtful. "Sounds like a herd of cows after they shot the last wolf," he said at last.

The Fabian reaction is said to have been too much to repeat in polite company.

The incident probably didn't happen, but it should have.

THE WEB
OF THE
CHOZEN

One

Ghosts are almost always malevolent and should be given a clear berth.

This particular ghost was over four kilometers long, a giant oval orbiting a planet circling a yellow sun. Only one kind of spaceship was ever built that large: a generation-ship from centuries past, before Igor Kutzmanitov discovered how to bend space right around the laws of relativity. A large number of such ships had been launched in the twenty-first century, carrying everything needed to start a new colony on some hoped-for Earth-like planet out there in the void. Most had been crewed by members of political or religious groups, searching for worlds of their own with the dedication necessary to reach out across time and space, knowing that they probably wouldn't live to see the promised land themselves.

I punched up the silhouette on my information screens. The ship's computer matched it—somewhat to my surprise, since these scouts don't exactly have the master library of Lubriana on them—as a Type IV Generation Ship, launched between 2140 and 2165, probably by an American or West European group, complement at start-off between two and three hundred with at least five master controllers in deep freeze. As to the actual identity—well, the computer said that seven such ships of that model were launched, and all were utopians of one sort or another. Beyond that it couldn't go.

I punched in some figures, curious as to how long

1

the thing could have been parked here. The screen told me that it couldn't have been here more than fifteen or twenty years at the outside, perhaps less than that.

That would mean that the odds were good that as many as all five of the original masters would be still alive.

I sighed and turned to look at the blue-green planet on my port screens. I was paid to find Earth-like or Terraformable worlds; if this one was taken, then there were no gold stars for Bar Holliday on this stop. Seiglein Corporation hardly needed to go at it with a bunch of utopians.

Even so, I would be expected to do a complete report. There was always the slim possibility of a profit in any discovery, even one like this, and while I'd get a zero for the discovery I'd get pilloried but good for failing to follow up.

I flipped open the communications lines and tried a scatter frequency that should have hit whatever twenty-first-century communications device they were using. The little red light on the panel lit up, announcing a lock, and I called the ship, not really expecting an answer. Even so, there might still be some people on board—or a relay to ground. The ship was in position for a relay if one there was.

"This is Seiglein Scout 2761XY," I called in my most professional manner. "Come in, generation-ship. Acknowledge, please."

There was only a hiss in return, and I repeated the message several times until I was satisfied that the store was empty.

Well, next step in the manual was to go aboard and check things out personally. I didn't particularly relish this idea since the damned thing was bigger than some cities, but regulations were regulations, and Seiglein's regulations book was Holy Writ.

The air lock on the big mother wasn't compatible, of course. It wouldn't be. However, I was able to establish a magnetic link near the lock, giving me only a meter or so to the lock itself, and I could play with the frequencies until I hit one the lock would recognize. In thirty minutes I was suited up, ready to go, and had both locks open. I prayed their automatics would still work; it would be hell to cut through the bulkhead to get in.

Only seconds after I cleared the big ship's lock, the door slid noiselessly shut behind me, and I felt the pressure normalizing. I looked at the monitor strapped to the outside of my pressure suit and saw that the air was still good. That made me feel better, and substantiated the argument that the ship hadn't been here all that long.

Well, they'd cleaned it out but good. Only the remains of the hydroponics tanks and the animal breeders and such were left. The rooms were empty of personal effects the crew and passengers would take with them, and all was doom and gloom.

The lights still worked, though. As per regulations the standby generators were on so that there was the possibility, however slim, of a quick getaway for colonists who ran into trouble.

There was no sign of anything like mutiny so they'd made it intact. Things looked really good. I tried to get at the bridge log to find out something about the crew and its origin, but the controls were out of a museum; I couldn't figure out how to work the damned computer.

There was, however, the usual plaque. Every crew mounted one next to the ship's construction-data plate, as if their new home were now a hallowed national monument or something. Which, I suppose, it was—to them.

The ship's data plate said it was the *Peace Victory,* built by Corben Yards on Luna from parts made in such-and-so U.S.A. and Canada, launched July 21, 2163—maybe the last of these babies, I thought.

The commemorative plaque was a little more informative, although not much.

"Peace Victory," it read, "brings the Communards to the place where they might found the society all mankind justly craves but cannot find under the fascist governments of Earth, no longer home. From this spot began the fulfillment of mankind."

I searched my memory, but couldn't remember anything about anybody called Communards. Commun*ists* I knew—we had lots of those—but Communards? A variation, maybe? It was at times like these that I regretted sleeping through my history classes all those years—if the movement had been big enough and rich enough to fund a generation-ship they must have been mentioned there.

Oh, hell, I thought. Communard comes from *community* and *common,* meaning they were a group society of some kind, mutual cooperation and all that, sharing all. Probably a damned dull bunch—almost certainly not a bar on the planet.

I made my way back down the empty corridors, the soles of my pressure-suited feet clanging in the atmosphere that procedure said I still couldn't breathe. I got lost twice and had to take advantage of a couple of *You Are Here* diagrams etched into the ship's walls to make it back to the right lock.

It was there that I saw a sign I hadn't noticed on entering, one that made me suddenly a bit more nervous and apprehensive.

On the door of the lock somebody had used a really hard tool or something to scrawl a crude *Don't.*

Don't what? I wondered. Don't go? Don't follow? Or was it just somebody's idea of a joke?

I looked around, but that's all there was. That one lonely, crude *Don't* and nothing more.

Well, I did anyway.

Two

Scouting is a lonely job, and I'm not the kind of person who normally likes being cooped up and isolated. Occasionally, both at home or on some other planet, people ask me why I'm in this line of work.

It's really hard to explain. For one thing, there is what I must call, for want of a better term, the flyer's mentality. Something in me loves to fly these things, loves to go out among the stars and see them the way no one else sees them, to poke into esoteric corners nobody imagined existed, to experience sights others see only in fictionalized dramas. Maybe that's it, too— there's a little of the hero and the ham in every pilot I've ever known, even the milk-run ferryboat people.

And then, too, it's so damned *dull* back home. Now they've got one's expected lifespan up past three hundred years, more than two-thirds of it in near-guaranteed good health, and the best free social services around. Nobody *has* to work, and many don't. They're born, live their lives in the same community where they're born, in government flats on the not uncomfortable government dole, sitting around talking about all the big things they're going to do and never get around to doing. Those who *do* something, who like to push buttons and things and people around, they're in the managerial government or in the nine corporations that keep the resources flowing, provide the services, and thereby run the lives of just about everybody.

I don't know why I turned out different. Bar 31-

626-7645 Holliday, raised in Seiglein's Total Care Center #31 along with a couple hundred other infants, was always different. Like all kids, I dreamed—but I dreamed beyond the time of settling, of puberty, and the dole. I guess in some ways I never grew up. I was good-looking, athletic, never any problems with the opposite sex, but I was troubled by things that others weren't. I'm not sure what—I often think of those days and wonder. One thing is that I was never satisfied with anything other than first place in the things that interested me—particularly sports. I was competitive, no doubt about that. And the Seiglein Corp. loved that kind of oddball, encouraged him, nurtured him, until they had put him right where they wanted him.

Maybe that was it—here I was, out in the middle of nowhere, looking into places nobody else had been before.

First.

To find some more resources for the billions on the dole on the hundreds of worlds, to find more worlds to house more billions who would turn them into more plastic places.

That was a system?

I don't know. Somehow I always thought of Seiglein and the other corporations as being in the vegetable-growing business.

Well, I wasn't a vegetable, or, if I was, I was a unique kind of vegetable.

Out here, the only one in charge of my welfare and destiny was me, the way it used to be in the old days, the way I'm convinced it ought to be.

I fed the data on the *Peace Victory* into the scout's computer and stared again at that pretty world out there. Looked a lot like Earth was supposed to look —I'd never been there, but I'd seen pictures. Definitely the best prospect I'd ever found, and, dammitall, somebody else found it first.

Well, next step was to survey the place in preparation for landing.

Those Communards, whatever they were, sounded like ripe candidates for Seiglein Products.

Still, that scrawled *Don't* on the inside of the air lock bothered me. Something kept nagging at me inside, and I decided that this one would be played safe. Budget be damned, I was going to scout this place as if there were nobody home.

I set up and shot a survey probe down to the planet. Hell, I couldn't even name it—they'd already named it somewhere. A little less immortality for Bar Holliday this time around.

The probe broke, leveled off at about 10,000 meters, and started doing a survey. The optics were quite good, and the magnification was superb. I could find out most of what I wanted to know from my command chair.

The thing started shooting stop-frames every three seconds, and I got a look at this world. It looked nice, even sort of familiar. Four big continents with irregular coastlines, huge blue oceans, vast plains broken by large lakes and rivers, and a number of tall mountain ranges. Even spotted a few volcanoes, so the place was still very much alive and active.

I hadn't seen any signs of human life as yet, but that was to be expected. At this stage I wasn't looking for people, and even if *Peace Victory* had been parked for twenty years there wouldn't be very many folks there yet, just some still getting along on the stuff from the ship, others living a primitive, self-reliant life in the best spots.

The place was warm; the south polar cap was small despite calculations that said it was winter; in summer, it probably vanished completely. The axial tilt was about nine degrees, not enough to cause severe seasons anyway. The mountains in both hemispheres had snow, though it was a little more pronounced in the southern hemisphere.

I shifted the probe to the commercial spectrum, and whistled. Lots of nice stuff down there still in the ground—they sure had the resources for a nice little world.

Heavy forests in the north and south, but a broad band around the center, about forty degrees on either side of the equator, seemed to be tropical savanna broken only by the mountain ranges. North Pole temperature −4° C. South Pole −9°, not bad at all. Equator was hot—over 50 degrees C, but the savannas generally ranged from about 20 to a high of 29. Very good.

They'd reached the land of milk and honey, all right. I tried to imagine them as they first explored it, probed it, realized what they had, and excitedly got ready to found their perfect society or whatever it was. If they had gods, they were definitely on their side.

I took a mid-savanna frame and held it, blew it up in register until I could have seen a pinhead on the plains.

Animals. Lots of them. Damned weird ones.

Took about two hours to get a really good, clear shot of them, unblurred and in perspective, but when I did I had to stare.

Now, I've been around a lot of the unknown universe. So far we haven't found any alien civilizations or really intelligent beasties, but the animal and plant life has been roughly logical. This place was so close to Terranorm that I half expected to see the usual animals—most of the plants *did* appear variations of existing types the environment would produce according to evolution's laws.

But these—well, they looked like they'd been designed by a committee that had debated what it was to be and never really decided. The creatures were a compromise.

Their heads were overlarge but somewhat humanoid, although rough-hewn. Long, thick whiskers, like a cat's, drooped down almost to the ground. Their ears—well, I'd seen donkeys in zoos, and that's about the closest I can come. Huge, long, almost a meter high, and they seemed to be able to turn them independently over at least a ninety-degree range. Two horns, fairly long, rose out of their heads above the eyes, terminating in flat membranes, purpose unknown. The male's horns were grand—they curved around once before straightening up again; the female's were straight and slightly shorter. And those eyes— weird. Jet black. No, I don't mean the pupils—the big eyes were like obsidian, from lid to lid.

Their bodies were equally incongruous. Again I have to go back to Earth animals I've seen in zoos and picture books. The body was like a giant kangaroo's, complete with massive hind legs which ended, not in big feet, but in large hooves, like horse's hooves. Their forelimbs were very long, since their bodies put them at an angle, but very horselike.

And all of this ended in a large, flat bushy tail, like a squirrel's, proportional to those bodies and fully as long.

I put the probe on hold and started watching a group of the beasts. They could stand erect, maybe two meters or more tall, resting on that tail, but to walk or eat they needed to be on all fours.

Did I say walk? Well, they hopped. Damnedest thing anybody ever saw. They would kick off with those hind legs and go real fast across the plain like a kangaroo, then settle on those forelegs. They couldn't walk as such—while the forelegs were independent of each other, the rear ones were locked together, obviously had to move together.

Their genitals looked to be oversized versions of the human type, but the females had no sign of breasts—although two large breastplates on both males and females suggested that they might once have had them. Both sexes also had large pouches below those plates, both carried young in them. Their bodies were covered by a greenish-blue fur, their faces a dark brown.

They were herbivores for sure—they would kneel and start chomping with great appetite on various plants. Flat teeth, a side-to-side chewing motion, and large, flat tongues.

I stared at them for what must have been hours, wondering what could possibly produce such things. What conditions would develop them that way?

They had no hands, no tentacles, so they had no tools—yet they did have artifacts of a sort. I caught a frame of something weird and blew it up.

It was a village.

Yes, a village, huts and all. All made out of something white and milky, like spider's web but looking much, much tougher and stronger. These things lived in them.

And as I watched, fascinated, I saw how they built them. There seemed to be a flap in the tongue. They'd pucker their mouths, and stick out the tongue, and out would come stuff with the consistency of rope, but like paste. They could build with it—very quickly, too, I noted—and I couldn't imagine where the material to make the stuff was coming from. A byproduct of the grasses they ate, maybe?

Reluctantly I turned my attention to other animal life. It was there, of course—some of it as strange-looking as the herbivores, but much of it more conventional. All around were birds, and insects, and smaller animals of various kinds. None looked quite right, but none looked as wrong as the chief creatures of the plains.

The air check I'd made at the beginning showed the world to be more humid than Terranorm, but that was about it. Nitrogen, hydrogen, oxygen there in nice balance, just below normal—most of the deviation being extra hydrogen, which accounted for the wetter climate—and inert gasses in essentially meaningless fractional percentiles.

I could breathe the stuff without discomfort, except that it would probably feel like a wet blanket. No deserts of more than a few thousand kilometers, all on the lee side of mountains or on a few very high plateaus.

I dropped the probe for a complete sample, then sterilized it except for the little specimen compartment. Once back, it was put through its paces in a vacuum chamber, probed, prodded, and analyzed much as the colonists must have done.

The usual types of microorganism. Nothing looked threatening.

Next came the search for the colony itself.

I sent the probe back out, and did a complete habitation survey. I found lots and lots of those web villages, and lots and lots of herbivores, but no indication of any human habitation whatsoever. After almost a day and night in probe status, I hadn't uncovered the slightest sign that human beings had ever landed on the planet.

Suddenly that scrawled word crept back into my conscious mind.

I was about to scoot back to the nearest relay station and get some advice—and maybe some heavy scientific artillery—when I suddenly remembered that twenty-first-century ships used nuclear fuel. Well, there was a lot of uranium and such here, but if their ship had landed, repeatedly landed, in a single spot I could find it. I ran one last probe on that guess, and hit pay-dirt.

The patterns were there, all right—big overlapping circles of weak radiation, and an indication of a small amount of something hot that was just about what their power pack would be.

But no sign of people around anywhere, and no sign of the ship that power pack should belong to.

I decided to get some sleep and continue when I was refreshed. A mystery was here, deep and unusual, and I knew that the odds were that I shouldn't try it myself. Even so, it's in my nature to try any problem.

11

If I could solve this one I would have more Seiglein feathers to add to my cap. Here was a challenge, and I never could resist challenges.

I knew I'd go down in full suit and armor to take a look.

But why did my mind insist on flashing that contradictory scrawled message to me as I made that decision?

Don't, it said.

The next day I sent down the bioprobe with a nurd inside. A nurd is a small organism from one of the Altarian planets that resembles nothing so much as a little rubber ball. That's about all it is, too—oh, not rubber, but it's biochemistry, while strange, is simple and the variables can be easily isolated. The things store in the deep freeze, too, and are susceptible to almost all diseases that might affect people—just about the perfect lab specimen.

The probe landed near the radiation zone and picked up some soil and air samples. The probe also let the nurd drop, bounce, and then neatly caught it again and popped it back inside. I immediately triggered the takeoff sequence, and while the liftoff friction sterilized the outside I ran the inner sterilization sequence so that only the tiny biological chamber, now suspended in a vacuum, remained from the planet.

Once back aboard, the automatic lab analyzed, probed, and poked here and there. It took about an hour to give some results.

The place was filthy with microorganisms, of course, but none of them seemed able to survive in the nurd. Nice. And normal. Rarely do the organisms of one world have any real effect on those of another, unless it's a lethal one. Only one organism, which was almost unnoticed it was so microscopic, seemed to have any compatibility factor at all with the nurd or with people, and that was a very primitive virus of some sort.

Blown up several million times, it barely showed on the screens. It didn't die or run from the nurd's cells, but neither did it seem to have any effect on the little ball-like creature. Like most of its type, it resembled a small honeycomb. It *did* seem to be a fast grower—I could see little sprouts off the ends of the colony slowly inch their way up what might have been a fraction of a micron—yes, it was that minute—and slowly form a new little protocell. This was much more rapid than anything I'd observed before—usually you can't see it happening, you just come back later and more of them have shown up—but after a few hours it seemed to reach the limits of its growth in the nurd and turned dormant. There was no effect on the nurd's temperature, biochemistry, or other vital functions, so it was probably safe for me as well.

But then, that Communard colony would have done much the same thing, been just as careful, and yet—where was it?

Everything checked out, and so now came the last-resort decision—turn for home and help, or go on down myself. Something in me said repeatedly that I should get out, but my stubborn, adventuring streak took over. I had been challenged here—somewhere down there should be a colony, thousands of people by this time, maybe farms, roads, and the like. Even if something unforeseen had wiped them out, there should be artifacts—shuttle ships were *tough*. Anything that could totally destroy one would be so damned obvious nobody would land.

Well, they'd landed. Down there. On that spot. Were they hidden, perhaps? Underground? I'd have to go down to find out.

I surveyed the area again. A broad, flat plain at the base of low, rolling mountains. There, two rivers formed valleys, came together in high grasslands, then still shallow and rocky, began to meander into a flood plain.

A large herd of the impossible herbivores was graz-

ing on the plains, and the area was rich in other wild-
life as well. I decided that I would not try the patience
of those weird-looking, grass-eaters; their legs had
tremendous muscles, and could probably break every
bone in my body without any trouble.

The creatures continued to bother me; they had no
right or justification in this setting. Something nagged
at the back of my mind, but I couldn't bring it forward;
something I'd seen that related to all this. I had to
let it sit, hoping it would come out when it was ready.

I still had a mystery here, and I didn't want to
chance those microorganisms no matter what they
did or didn't do to the nurd, so I suited up and took
an eight-hour supply of air—it was all recirculated
but the size of the initial supply and the filtration made
the limits—and my portapack, which would link me
with the computer on the ship and its analytical facili-
ties.

I touched down on the plain near the spot where
the last of the mountains met the river. Animals scat-
tered, probably fearing the whine of the large object
settling down among them more than the object itself. I shut off the drive and moved to the air lock,
feeling my usual extreme discomfort at suddenly having full gravity again after a long period at half-*G*.

Here it *was* one *G*—no, not exactly. A little more,
but close enough. It was always a shock to my system, though, to remember suddenly how much weight
it had been carrying for so long.

The outer lock opened with a whirring sound and I
lowered the little steps to the ground. There was no
danger in leaving the door open; the inner door
was solidly shut, and the computer would respond only
to my own codes.

The ground was soft, slightly muddy, probably from
a recent rain. It rained quite often around here, and
the grass, a blue-green, was extremely tall and vibrant-
looking.

I immediately saw why the native animal life had

such tough skins, though—the grass blades were very sharp, and would be a problem to anything without protection. Near the base of the adult grass were several slightly munched tubers or growths the consistency of potato or apple inside. Although they were hard and not easily crushed, they were apparently another part of the diet of the herbivores.

I stopped and looked around carefully. The instruments said that their shuttle had landed, not once but many times, near this very spot—yet there wasn't a sign of a ship that had to be a great deal larger than my own not inconsiderable craft.

Nothing.

Some of the animals had ventured back into my landing zone. Their curiously humanoid faces were uplifted, and some were sitting upright on their bushy tails staring at me with those strange, all-black, glassy eyes of theirs. They didn't make a sound other than when moving around, but their long ears were obviously turned to me and the funny membranes on top of their horns quivered slightly.

I had the distinct impression that I was being watched.

Suddenly feeling a bit nervous and overexposed, I checked my pistol for full charge. I made my way cautiously to the river, which broke the grasslands with a line of trees and an orange-brown, sandy soil.

The river itself rushed and gurgled along, perhaps a kilometer wide but only fifteen or twenty centimeters deep.

The feeling of being watched persisted; and I had been around enough to trust my instincts. I whirled around and saw that the creatures of the plain were following me, still looking at me with rather too much intelligence and still maintaining about a fifty-meter distance.

Near the river were other, more normal-seeming animals. One looked like a tiny mule, another looked something like a squirrel although it had a long snout and was obviously semiaquatic.

Something that looked like a meter-tall hare skipped rapidly through the brush, so comically I chuckled in spite of my tension. It looked like what the big herbivores *should* look like.

There was another animal, somewhat pig-faced but with long, menacing horns, and its nasty expression proved a bluff as it ran squealing when I approached. Insects of various kinds buzzed around, and there were a few types of bird, although they looked more like lizards and seemed to do more gliding than flying as they ate the insects.

Two things struck me: the lizard-birds were the first carnivores I'd seen on this planet, anywhere—and, except for the buzzing of the insects, the rushing of the river, and the rumbling of a light wind, there were no sounds.

The place reminded me of a game preserve, protected and well managed. Yes, that was it—a game preserve for nonpredators. But—if so, what kept the population in check? And who ran it?

I walked into the river, watching my step on the rocks the fast-moving water was slowly pushing downstream, and started heading up to the split. That would be where *I* would start my first town and center if I'd landed as a colonist.

The big herbivores didn't venture into the water, but they did slowly pace me along the bank. I could see them trying to slow-hop, or drag their heavy bodies along by the power of their front legs alone.

There *was* a settlement on the point where the two rivers met, but it wasn't a human one. It was one of the curious villages the herbivores built out of spit. Closer up, it looked even more impressive—a broad main street, a network of small buildings constructed with infinite care, many of them looking to be the same kind of standard one-room dwelling; a few others larger and grander, one even having a point and two subsidiary spires.

Sooner or later, I knew, I would have to face them, but I preferred not to at this stage. I needed to know more, as unaggressive as every animal here seemed. I stopped.

The herbivores bothered me for reasons other than their looks. All evidence said they were somewhat intelligent; the village looked as if it had been thought out rather than built by instinct. Their actions toward me seemed intelligent, too. And yet—well, everything I'd ever been taught about exobiology said that without the ability to handle tools the evolution of a complex intelligence was impossible.

But was it?

I seemed to recall that back on Earth they'd had some kind of sea mammal, a dolphin I think it was, with intelligence, language, a large brain—and nothing but its mouth. But that animal had developed in a stimulating environment; it was soft like people, had to live in a medium that could kill it as easily as it could kill me, and had lots of predatory enemies. It had to outthink that sort of environment or die.

No such pressures existed here. Plenty of food, fine climate, no predators.

Then suddenly that nagging, pestering thought that wouldn't focus became clear. Those creatures *were* designed by a committee, a committee with very little imagination. I had seen most of the disparate, component elements of their bodies—the horns, the tail, the long ears, the hind-leg arrangement—in terms of other animals. I would probably also find an animal that built by spitting silk somewhere, and marsupials of various kinds all over. The forelegs were based on the mule.

Those creatures had been assembled from patterns drawn from the natural denizens of this world.

They hadn't evolved, they'd been made up.

They were somebody's biology experiment.

17

It was hard to believe, I didn't *want* to believe it, but there it was. Whoever had done this was damned good if not overly creative. The colony—*those herbivores were the colony!*

"Oh, my God!" I breathed aloud, both in wonder and in fear.

This *was* somebody's game preserve, and if you moved in you were incorporated into it.

I suppressed my panic and thought things through. Supposing these creatures *were* the colony? They could hardly have populated the planet in the single generation they'd been here, even if they had a dozen young every month or two. No, the number in this colony was right, but where did the millions of others across eighty degrees of latitude come from?

Maybe I was lacking part of the puzzle after all.

I decided to take the bull by the horns and go back to the ship and try to face down my curious but distant companions. Given their intelligence, it might be possible to establish some sort of contact.

I made my way back down the river and eventually spotted my tracks on the bank. Coming through the trees, I was back on the plain—and stopped.

There was a new mountain where the ship had been left; consisting of the hard spittle web these creatures spun, it rose in a huge dome.

They had completely sealed the ship in the stuff in the two short hours I'd been gone.

Thoughts of contact forgotten, I got mad. I didn't like being played for a sucker, and I wasn't going to let anybody get away with it. I walked up to the milky-white wall and pushed.

It was hard as a rock.

Well, okay, then, I thought, determined, I have something that will go through a rock.

Standing off to avoid any sort of beam splatter, I put the pistol on full blast and fired its blue-white lightning at the shell.

I could see an area start to darken, a little smoke

rising up. The stuff *was* tough, but it could be broken.

Suddenly the pistol stopped firing. Puzzled, I looked at it, and examined its charge meter. There should have been a half-hour's worth in there, but there wasn't. The meter was dead.

And, so, in fact, was the pistol. I watched in horrible fascination as the plastic corroded before my eyes. On impulse I squeezed and the thing crumbled like so much pumice.

Mad and scared, I took out the portapack and told the computer to take off.

The portapack was corroding before my eyes as I tried to send the codes. Within seconds it was useless; within minutes it was in the same condition as the pistol.

Suddenly my suit felt funny, and it became hard to breathe. I knew what it was—the agent that had nabbed the pistol and portapack was at the air-filtration system. Within another two or three minutes at most, I would have to get out of the suit, the air would just run out.

I screamed in fury, rushed to that web-wall separating me from my world, and banged my fist against the charred spot I'd made. As I did so, my gloves crumbled, and my hands were exposed to the outside air, yet I continued to pound in utter helplessness and frustration, making little cuts as I did so.

Nobody had ever beaten Bar Holliday before.

Three

In about an hour it was all gone. I sat there in the grass, naked, my head in my hands. Nothing remained of my own artifacts—all had crumbled to dust.

Something in me refused to admit defeat, even in the face of such unknowable, unguessable power. What could have caused the total destruction of my things? Particularly so quickly and completely? A ray? Nothing in the air surely—that had tested out pretty well.

Or did it? The tests had always been reliable before, sure, but they were still guesses. They tested only for things man had thought of, had imagined or encountered in the past. The computers couldn't answer questions that hadn't already been asked. That was why human beings were still sent out as scouts.

The trouble was, I thought grumpily, the humans had forgotten why they were sent. I was a creature of my devices, my machines—I depended on them utterly.

Now what? I wondered. Do I join the colony? How do they do that?

And who were "they"?

I got up, suddenly feeling hungry. The grass was the only thing around, but my system definitely wasn't made to eat it. I thought briefly of suicide, but that would be an admission of defeat. No, I couldn't do that—I couldn't give them the satisfaction. I was not defeated as long as life and thought remained in me, and I would survive somehow. But to survive I had to eat.

I looked at the tubers at the base of the plant, and with some difficulty, I pulled one free. They seemed edible—had a kind of nice, sweet taste, like a cross between a pear and a domesticated apple. Not bad, although a little hard to chew. I almost choked to death on a piece a little too big, and learned that I had to nibble.

Several of them went down, and they were wonderful. The more I ate, the more I wanted to eat, and I found myself consuming them as quickly and as greedily as I could find them until, finally, I was so stuffed that I could feel the backup in my throat.

I awakened suddenly, as if from a dream, and realized what I was doing. For the first time in I don't know how long, I thought of something other than eating.

Why?

What had induced that incredible hunger in me? And for what purpose? It was clear that nothing on this world happened by chance.

Then it came to me. Raw material. If I was to be changed into one of the herd, then raw material was needed to begin the conversion. I felt sure that I would continue to be hit by starvation spells that could only be satisfied by eating the tubers that would turn me into raw material for them to do with me what they wanted to do.

I looked around and saw many of the herbivores watching me intently, and I thought I could detect both sympathy and sadness on their all-too-human faces. Many of them must have gone through this as well, I realized. They understood.

I wondered how much they understood? Did they know, even now, what had done this to them?

I decided that now was the time to make contact, if possible, but when I started toward them I felt dizzy and eventually had to stop and sit in the grass, which stung as I settled.

I felt strange, funny—like I'd never felt before.

Not sick, really, but tremendously tired, disoriented. I wanted only to lie down in the grass and go to sleep, which I did.

The crash-boom of thunder and the pelting of rain-drops woke me. I was still in the field, but the sky was now ominously dark and a big storm was almost upon me. I got up and decided to make for the trees near the river, a place that would at least afford some shelter. I felt really good—not high, just excellent. I sprinted for the trees, still conscious of the stinging from the grass, and made it just before the big deluge hit the now-empty plains.

More or less protected by the trees, I settled back and examined myself. As far as I could see, I hadn't changed in any significant way. I relaxed a little, glad that I hadn't awakened a monster.

So what *had* changed? I wondered. Where had the mass of tubers gone?

The temperature had dropped dramatically with the storm, and I shivered a little in the chill, which was bad only if contrasted to the temperature before.

Suddenly I knew where *some* of the tubers had gone—I had to take a crap, badly, and I had to do it *au naturel*. Well, it wasn't the first time, although in the past I had always had more than cold water to clean up with afterward.

The storm lasted over an hour and then rumbled audibly along down the plain for some time. The area remained cloudy, though, and looked a little threat-ening, even though the temperature and humidity started to climb back up with astonishing rapidity.

Soon I was perspiring all over, and I felt as if I were covered by a thick, wet blanket. The situation obviously was still too threatening for the herbivores. Some of the other animals were out, but not them.

After about a half-hour, I decided to make my way down to the village. Before I could get started, though, I was starving again.

This time the orgy seemed to last much longer and included the grass as well as the tubers. Everything seemed to taste wonderful, and it was a long while before I could get enough of it. When my appetite subsided I was so stuffed that I finally had to spit out the remains of grass-and-tuber mush from my mouth. Having learned my lesson, this time I just sat down rather than trying any activity.

I knew I was right about one thing, though. The stuff that I was eating was to give the transforming agent something to work with. The fact that I ate the grass was in itself remarkable; the fact that it neither cut the insides of my mouth nor tasted bad at all was even more unusual. A great many changes had been wrought in me, all internal.

I wished I knew how long this nonsense would take. Obviously I could do nothing constructive until the process was completed. I resigned myself to it.

When I awoke the next time, it was morning. I had slept through the entire night—or had I been in some sort of coma?—and the clouds were now broken, the warm sun peeking through. The plains were again stirring with life.

Lying there, I wondered why none of the colony had yet come to me, tried to contact me. I was afraid for a moment that they couldn't, but, I asked myself, why should they? To what purpose, as long as this process was going on? Plenty of time later for introductions.

By this time some of the changes were external. I was starting to grow body hair of the greenish-blue hue I had noticed earlier, and my skin was turning darker and becoming tougher. The grass no longer stung me nor cut as it had. I had that exhilarated feeling again, euphoric, sort of. I felt neither hungry nor thirsty, but I made my way back down to the river, hoping to find some spot which would give me a reflection.

Scouts, it was said, were picked because they alone

possessed a thousand unique traits necessary to perform their duties; one, certainly, was the ability to accept and adjust to alien experience, something that, in this extreme circumstance, was surprising even me. I wondered sadly how many of that doomed colony had taken their transformation so calmly, how many had, perhaps, committed suicide or gone mad. It must have been a horrifying experience, first to see all of their possessions, their artifacts, dissolve about them, then to go through this slow, uncomfortable process.

Still, I didn't have a clue as to who was behind the transformation or how it was being done.

I searched the river bank for several hundred meters until I found a small pool of water isolated from the torrent by debris and still enough for a reflection. When at last I looked, there were changes indeed. My face had already begun to take on that broader cast, my mouth was wider, and, when I opened it, I discovered that my teeth were being replaced with larger, flatter ones. A little experimentation showed that I could chew from side to side. My tongue was much larger and thicker, a pale gray in color, and I could see the rather large flap at its tip. My arms were longer— my hands came down to my lower calf—and they seemed rounder, more sinewy.

Shortly thereafter that insatiable hunger came and I was off again. This time it was difficult to make my arms bend to feed myself, and I started taking in huge gobs of grass and grabbing tubers with my mouth. They were easier to eat now, and everything chewed better, went down smoother.

Again I slept, and when I awoke the sun was high overhead, the plains teeming with life, much of it watching me but making no move in my direction.

I tried to reach up to wipe the sleep from my eyes but found that my arms would no longer bend to that purpose, only back. I looked at them, and they were getting to be thick, long, horselike legs. My hands were lumps, not quite hooves as yet but on the way.

24

I was on my side, and rolled over, getting unsteadily to my feet—all four of them. The back ones only moved in unison now, and I wasn't constructed quite right to use them properly as yet, so I could only pull myself along unsteadily with my forelegs, down to the river again, to my still reflecting pool.

Things were developing fast now, I saw. My metabolism must be racing hundreds of times faster than normal. The only way this could be done was by some variant of cancer, some mutation inside each cell of my body which, when completed, stabilized and reproduced itself, discarding the old cells. I once heard it said that the human body completely replaced everything but its brain cells every seven years. My metabolism was enormously speeded up, I knew —that would explain the euphoric feelings, the constant fatigue, and the frequent spells of insatiable hunger. Everything worked out down to the smallest detail.

Well, they'd had a lot of practice.

My body hair and chest plate were complete now, I saw in the reflection, and my face was now fully that of the plains herbivore, although, curiously, it retained enough of me to be recognizable. The ears were taking shape, but seemed unformed at this point; there was, as yet, no sign of the horns or, I saw by twisting around, the tail.

Soon I was starving again, and it was back to the fields. I was like a robomower; kneeling, face practically in the dirt, I gobbled up tubers and grass at an amazing rate. I also gobbled some dirt and small pebbles, and it didn't seem to matter—in this state I could think only of eating.

I awakened again near dusk, noting that it had rained on me. Everything was wet, yet I'd slept through it all.

I was again on my side, a larger bulk than I'd started as, forelegs and the like now fully formed. I

25

found that the front hooves were not quite solid; they divided neatly into thirds with some movement possible. I could open to form a gap, then close on an object.

Not exactly hands, and neither could you grasp everything nor use it much once you had it, but I had *some* control. I was sure there was a reason for it.

I got up on all fours. The hind legs seemed firm and sure, and I decided to experiment a little. I kicked off and leaped a good ten meters, but came crashing down, unable yet to steady myself. It hurt, and I felt bruised and a little defeated, so I made sure to take it slow and careful thereafter. This running and jumping trick would take some practice.

I couldn't walk, but had to hop, and it took a lot of spills before I could do even a slightly fast jog without falling down. But I felt sure I'd have the movements down pat in a couple of days. I had to— it would be the only way I could get around.

I was also conscious of my ears. I could feel them —I could feel almost every part of my body—and I could move them, even independently.

And I heard.

Voices far off in the distance, high-pitched and oddly distorted, but I heard. There were a lot of such sounds—almost a cacophony of noise, impossible to sort out into its individual components.

Everything, I realized, made noises here.

That the ears were a lot more sensitive than my old ones I had no doubt, but why had this been a world of silence before? I considered that. Perhaps the sounds were all too high-pitched for human hearing? I hadn't really adjusted the suit for anything outside the human spectrum.

It was too dark to see what I looked like, even if I could get all of myself to the pool, so I decided to wait until the next hunger bout before worrying about it. I knew what I was going to look like when I was finished; I could only explore the body fully and learn its limitations when it was complete. I practiced running. Still not much of a tail, therefore so much for standing, but I could feel the beginnings back there. It wouldn't be long before I resembled the herbivores in this respect, too.

Although I had no way of telling time, it took an abnormally long period for the next eating spell to come on. Perhaps, near the end of the process, you started slowing down to normal.

When next I awoke, it was still dark. Strange that I could feel the warm sun on my back as I got up, yet I couldn't see a thing. Then it hit me:

I was blind.

There was no question about it. I could *hear* the life teeming around me, hear the rush of the waters off in the distance, hear the wind and the flying things overhead, the insects buzzing about.

But all was darkness.

I stood still on all four legs, trying to get my bearings. As tough as it had been to run the evening before, running blind would be impossible. These people *couldn't* be blind, I told myself. I had watched them moving, running, leaping—and they *built*. It must be some kind of change in the optic system, I thought desperately, remembering the strange eyes, like pieces of shiny, polished brown glass, that filled them.

The sounds were enormous; they seemed to flood in, confusing and consuming me. Even so, I could hear . . . voices.

Yes, voices definitely, but how far off I couldn't tell. Thin, reedy, high-pitched, but recognizable voices at that.

A crowd of them, all talking at once. It was a mob; there wasn't much chance that I could pick any one individual out.

I was conscious that the tail was in place now. I could wave it, bend it, make it freeze in any position. It was as long as my body, and bushy. I was conscious of a lot of insects buzzing around me and discovered that the thing was an effective device for brushing them away.

I wondered about the horns. I kneeled down and put my forehead almost to the ground. Yes, they were there, but short, stubby, and, to judge from pressing on them, crooked. Not quite in yet.

One more time, I thought to myself. One more and the job will be done. Once more and I'll be able to join the group, find out what's going on, make plans to free myself of this curse.

I stood there, trying to catch any part of the conversations going on around me. The language was familiar, and I did catch a few phrases here and there, but it wasn't much use.

I wanted to call out to them, but I decided to wait, wait for the final steps of the transformation. It was obvious that the herbivores were deliberately keeping away, but keeping an eye on me, until the process was complete.

Because I was blind and not able to do much of anything, I practiced sitting up on my tail a few times and took spill after spill. Finally I managed it, repeated it, did it a third time.

It produced some interesting sensations once you got the knack. The last thing I'd been thinking about up to now had been sex, but this standing up on hind legs and tail made a forceful point.

As I said, I was extremely aware of every part of my body. Most of us aren't—we're aware of our various parts only when we use them or abuse them. Not this body—you felt every muscle, every nerve, every appendage. This included the penis, which in the four-footed position wasn't much. Standing, the organ proved to be an extremely long bony tube, straight out, and switched to the ejaculation position automatically. Sex was obviously a stand-up affair here.

I could feel the heat of the sun shift a good deal

before I started to get the glimmerings of hunger. Eating blind using only your head and mouth is tough, but the starvation imperative, present to this time, was missing. Time, which had raced, now was dragging, and I ate only to get it over with.

I didn't eat nearly as much this time, nor quite to stuffing, and the process took some time. Even so, when I felt full, that familiar tiredness came on and I knew I was fading out for what might be the last time.

I looked forward to the rest, fearing only that I would wake up blind still.

Four

"You awake yet, young fellow?" a high, mellow voice asked, concerned.

I groaned and stirred a little, forgetting for a moment where and what I was. It was unlike coming down from the other sessions; I felt as if I had really been asleep this time, and I was a little shaky and achy.

I opened my eyes, gasped, and shut them again.

"Oh, my God!" I managed, my voice sounding odd to my ears.

"It takes some getting used to," the strange voice admitted. "You'll get the hang of it with practice. Might as well start—get to your feet and I'll help you."

I used the tail as a side brace and got unsteadily to my four feet. Again I opened my eyes and stared.

Once, as a small child, I had experienced a kaleidoscope—you turned the thing this way and that and got an ever-changing variety of strange shapes and colors. I'd seen similar effects done electronically by telescreen, too.

What I saw was like that, only infinitely more complex—and without clear borders. Some colors flashed and whirled and spun, some stayed put, and there were more shades and hues than I could imagine, a few so odd-looking that I could never have imagined them before. What I saw was a series of fuzzy impressions, though, without form or shape.

"Is this the way you see?" I asked my unknown companion. "Lord! What does it all mean?"

"It's actually a better system than the old one," the other replied. "It's just that your brain isn't used to or prepared to accept the different input. Look, want to focus? Turn in my direction now, and feel those horns on your head. Feel them? Good. Now concentrate on them."

I tried what the other said, and suddenly the world exploded. The colors became sharply outlined as odd, distinct shapes. I could count the blades of grass, see the tiny bugs moving—not as pictures, really. No, it's hard to explain. Shape, size, texture, distance—all there, yet not optically. It still looked strangely electronic, totally unreal.

The other, now—I focused on him, seeing him in three dimensions yet not seeing him at all. He looked a pale blue, like a negative, though, and while I could literally count his body hairs and see how long each was, he seemed to be drawn on a telescreen which was constantly holding only a brief image and then being completely redrawn.

"No, it's not *seeing*," he commented, reading my wonder and puzzlement. "You're sending out thousands of tiny pulses per second from those membranes on top of the horns, and these are being returned to your ears and fed to the optic centers of your brain. Move your ears to the side and you'll see."

I did as he suggested, and the sharp images faded into color blurs directly in front of me, and new images started forming at the periphery of my vision, with less and less of the color in them. When my ears were rotated as far around as I could manage, the images to either side were uncolored, stark electronic white etched on pure black.

I brought my ears back around, and the colorful imagery returned to focus.

"The eyes are extremely color-sensitive, far into the ultraviolet and infrared," the creature explained, "but have nothing for definition. That's provided by the sonar, which is nondirectional and works for a hundred and eighty degrees in front of you. Just turn your ears to catch any part of the signal. That gives shape to the colors, and gives you extremely accurate depth perception. The only cost is in fine detail—you won't see much in the way of small detail unless you focus strictly on a small area. I probably look a solid blue to you, yet when you stared hard you saw the tiniest hairs on my body to the exclusion of the whole image. You can look close-up or panoramic, but not both."

"This is incredible," I managed, and it was. Things looked strangely alien, artificial. Objects faded in and out, outlines were sometimes clear, sometimes shaky. Interestingly, I could not see the horizon or the sky—they remained a dark blank against which the shapes and colors were etched.

"Where's the horizon?" I asked.

"Doesn't reflect sound. You'll see everything that you get an echo on; everything else just doesn't exist. Don't worry—you'll get used to it."

"The grass was blue-green," I noted. "Now it looks pink."

"That's a food color," my guide responded. "The colors don't really correspond to anything you'd have seen with your eyes. Everything pink you eat. There are subtle details you'll learn as you go along. For example, blue is a male color, green a female one. All sorts of signals—thousands of them. In a few weeks you'll know most by reflex or experience."

I shook my head. All of this bothered me. Being an alien was bad enough, but being *this* alien was more than I could accept. It put additional roadblocks in the way of my ever breaking the bonds that held me, of beating the system. I had the uneasy feeling that this was the purpose of much of the design—it met all your basic needs, but severely limited any attempt to break out of the preordained social structure. Those colors—they built habit patterns.

"You're from the Communard colony, aren't you?" I asked the man, trying not to dwell too much on dark thoughts. I was in a trap, and much needed to be learned if I was ever going to break out.

The man nodded. "Yes, I am George Haspinol, one of the masters for the trip. We divided up the place into districts, tried to get things in at least a rough social organization. It's worked, after a fashion, although we've spread so much now that I have no idea if all the original institutions still exist. We've been here a long time."

"You saw me come in, didn't you? Why have you waited until now to make contact?"

"Wouldn't have done much good before. When you stepped out onto Patmos you were already committed, too late to back out. We knew what would happen. You couldn't have heard us anyway—so why bother? After you started changing, your body rate, time rate, and such were so altered that you were out of sync with us. When I saw the horns start, I came over and kept a vigil. Plenty of time for talk now, anyway. That's the thing we have the most of here."

"You called the place Patmos," I noted. "That *your* name?"

The man's blue altered slightly to show some emotion. "Of course!" he responded. "You mean you never heard of Patmos? It's in the Bible."

I nodded. I knew what the Bible was, but hadn't ever read it. As I said before, I slept through my history classes.

George interpreted my silence with the perception that made him a master.

"I can see, then, that Christianity's fallen in the march of civilization," he said sadly. "Well, it was inevitable. One of the reasons the Communards left."

"So you were religious, not political," I responded. "With the name Communard I'd assumed—"

"Communism?" he sniffed. "Well, in the purest sense of the term, yes. We shared much of the same philosophy and goals, but differed with them on matters of the spirit. Both dreamed of a world without want, violence, or fear, where all would have enough and live in peace and equality forever. It's just that we could never accept the promise of fundamental change in human nature from within; we felt that a change could only come through God's grace. Communism is in itself a religion, with holy books, a god figure, prophets galore to interpret him, and a heaven which would come from a sudden, miraculous, scientifically unfounded change in human nature. Our changes, of the spirit, were far more logical and believable, I think."

I kept looking around, testing out my new vision. It was damned strange in what it did and didn't give you, and in its flexibility.

"So you came here and got trapped," I said sourly.

"Depends on how you look at it," replied the other. "Many of us believe that all of this is God's will, the only way to attain the paradise which we seek. In a way, they may be right—utopia means no violence, and none is here. Utopia means no wants or needs, and none are here. There is little pain here, the body heals itself quickly when injured, and death so far has been an isolated phenomenon. Many of us are happy here, and praise God constantly for this life."

"Hmph!" I snorted. "That's the trouble with utopias. When you reduce the ideal world to its basics, you find it fits a herd of cows very well. Is this what man strives for? To be reduced to a bunch of contented, grazing animals? I don't believe it. That's why I didn't stay home and rot on the lifelong dole; I had to explore, to meet and beat challenges wherever they could be found. That's humanity, *I* think."

George shrugged. "Maybe. Maybe not. Certainly if most of civilization is as you say they'd be better off grazing here on the plain. I make no judgments, since it's all academic anyway. I came to that conclusion long ago, and you will, too, sooner or later. You're here, like this, and you're stuck forever whether you want to be or not."

"I'll never accept that," I told him. "I'd rather die."

"Lots *did* try to kill themselves at the start, you know," he said softly. "It doesn't work. They won't allow it. Go crazy in any way and you get an instant lobotomy—there are lots like that out here. As you'll find out, we're functional pets—property."

"Of whom?" I asked. "Who's *they?*"

"Enough time for that later," George replied. "All the time in the world. I'm delighted to have somebody fresh and different to talk to. Right now let's go on up to the town and get you settled in. Can you run with this vision? Just take it as slowly as you can and don't try pushing it. I'll pace you, and try to guide you."

I tried running and found myself sprawling time and again. I couldn't get used to my new vision because movement caused everything to be even more confusing and disorienting than it seemed before. George moved as effortlessly as a four-legged ballet dancer, and I envied him his grace and balance. I wasn't sure I'd ever get to that point.

But he was always there, always shouting encouragement, and we eventually made it to the edge of the river.

Water was gold, like molten lava that somehow sparkled as it poured over ultraviolet rocks. The village looked different now, too, the buildings a glistening silver as intricately constructed as the most complex spiderwebs.

"This was the first town site," George explained. "It could have held the original six hundred easily, and we actually got some prefab stuff up before things started to fall apart. The earliest buildings on the point there are patterned after the ones we built, even the church."

So that was the building with spires, I thought. A church. I'd seen a couple on various worlds, but this sort of organization came out of ancient history. But, then, these *were* a people of ancient history, taking centuries to cover what I had covered in months. I was as alien to these people as we all were to normal humans—four hundred and seventy years distant.

"Of course," George continued, "as the population has expanded, we have spread far beyond the original site—now very far beyond. There's only a few thousand of us around in these parts, in three towns."

"A few *thousand* of you?" I gasped. "But you said you started with six hundred! You can't have been down twenty years!"

"That's true," he acknowledged. "But, you see, every single one of the Chozen—that's what we call this particular animal we are—on this planet started with the original six hundred."

I was stunned anew. "You mean—there were *no* creatures like this on this planet before you landed? That's impossible! There must be a billion of you around on all four continents! Not in twenty years!"

George sat up on his tail and gave a shrug. "It's true. When we surveyed, the largest land animal around was a large rodent, and the largest animal period was something resembling an aquatic dinosaur. We split into four groups, centered on each continent's best zone, to check where the best places would be to start out. Seventy-five men and seventy-five women in each commune, each with a whole continent to settle. We had radios and the shuttlecraft, so we could keep in contact, we thought. Well, after we were all down, the dissolution of everything started, so rapidly and so absolutely that we couldn't do a thing about it. Then the Change came, and, if I can judge by just this colony here, when we became the Chozen only one in ten of the men remained a male, the rest became females. In our case, seven of us remained men; the rest, females—sixty-eight in all.

"Breeding is—well, you might say compulsory. You'll see. A female mates once every two years, I'd guess, and always lays six eggs—yes, don't start. We hatch.

"Well, five are always female and one male. There's

no infant mortality to speak of, and instead of the usual ten to thirteen years, the young reach full maturity in just two and start breeding. You can figure out the result."

It was getting late as we approached the large house, which, as leader, George occupied. It was grass-lined and stocked with tubers, and provided a comfortable place to lie down in. The Chozen relaxed by lying on their sides, feet out, I found. Very comfortable.

My old pilot's mind did the arithmetic. Let's see—okay, there would be sixty-eight females, seven males, so we'd multiply the first litter by six and the rest by five. That was 408 the first breeding cycle, two years in. Now they all bred, and we'd get 2,040 by the end of the fourth year. Ten thousand two by six, fifty-one thousand by eight, two hundred fifty-five thousand at ten years, over a million two by only twelve years, six million at fourteen, thirty-one million by sixteen, a hundred and sixty or so million by eighteen, and now, at about twenty years, almost eight hundred million from this one colony. Multiplied by the four colonies, the result was even more staggering—over three billion of the Chozen on the planet. And the next cycle—

Fifteen billion?

"I don't believe it," I whispered. "This world's about right now. It can't stand any more inhabitants. You'll be out of food no matter what in just a couple more years, over the trillion mark before another decade!"

George nodded. "I know. The death rate's mostly from accident, so it's rather low. Either that has to increase dramatically in the next year or two, or there has to be a lot of sterility suddenly, or we'll be up to our tails in people with no increase in food."

"Starvation will return violence to your perfect world," I pointed out. "The most dangerous people are starving people."

Five

In the next few days I learned to handle my new body and my odd new sight much better. The fact is, being of the Chozen was not at all unpleasant, like suddenly becoming a child again. No cares, no responsibility, no worries. Most of the Chozen were born this way, and all but a handful were still children.

The young grew to adulthood in just two years, but they learned very quickly. Parents taught them speech and as much else as possible during the abbreviated childhood. Even as adults, they respected their elders, and listened to the stories of their heritage, their culture, and their ideals and faith. To all but a hundred and fifty of the colony, and those stretched damned thin across the face of the continent, this was their own, their only world, their only form, their only life. Legends, rumors, and the lack of manpower to fill what little need for knowledge of the old ways existed were already causing tremendous gaps between old and young. There were simply too many children, of necessity too spread out. Most were primitive savages, with little or no hint of a link to humanity or civilization.

They played their games, and life was fun and little else. I could tell that even close in to this village and George's guiding hand the last links were already breaking. Two years wasn't enough to teach them their past. Already the majority of the inhabitants were only two to four years old, and far removed from humanity. In a century, provided—or, perhaps, even helped by

—the inevitable toll of starvation, they would be so alien, so simple and primitive, that they might as well have no link with humanity whatsoever.

In one way, the originals would have the advantage in a fight. They'd know how to fight, would know about violence and how to defend. But, of course, their Christianity and pacifistic ideals would be shattered in the process; they would have to give up their dream or die for it. Either way, the process of dehumanizing would advance.

I talked to a bunch of young ones, just coming on two but already looking as adult as any of us. George had two daughters and a son from the last breeding cycle. One of the girls seemed brighter and more curious than the others, and I took a liking to her. They called her Guz—George explained that after so many kids he just called them simple names he could keep straight.

As I say, we were all children again, playing games like tag and hide-and-seek and such between bouts of eating—a lot had to be consumed each day to support our bulks. Guz was happy and alert, and you would have put her as an ignorant twelve-year-old big for her age if you didn't know better. Even with a master for a teacher, though, she was one of the new generation.

"Ay! Bar!" she taunted. "No can run quick like girl!"

I took the challenge and started after her; I was getting better every day, sprinting probably twenty kilometers per hour, maybe better. It *was* a tempting, deceptive paradise, really—no cares, no worries, all fun and games.

I *did* catch her and swatted her with my tail. She stopped and laughed, because she'd slowed deliberately to let me catch her and knew that I knew.

After a while of such romping about we ate our fill of grass and tubers, then settled in for the ritual that was part of everybody's day: people who knew each other would settle down and preen and clean one another. Basically, the process involved one person's lying down, while the other went over him, checking for burrs, insects, and the like, and removed them with tongue and teeth. Our mouths secreted an antiseptic saliva that healed rough and raw spots.

I took a couple of minutes, then started doing her.

"Bar?" she asked lazily. "What it like where you come from? What it like to be old people?" By that last she wasn't referring to age, but to the human form.

"I'm sure your father's told you all about it," I responded. "It is quite different."

"How?" she persisted, as all children must.

"Well, we have hands. We can grasp things—hold things," I tried to explain, realizing that "grasp" and "hold" might be hard concepts for a handless person. "We use tools—things that are used to make and shape other things."

"Why?"

That age-old question seemed a bit harder somehow. Why, indeed?

"Are people more happy than Choz?" she asked, filling the void of my nonreply.

I thought again, of the mindless millions glued to their telescreens and rotting in standard flats. I compared them to the happy primitives of the plains.

"I guess not," I replied carefully. "It's not a question of better, only different."

"What kind of different?" she persisted.

I finished the preen. "Sun's going down," I evaded. "Let's head for town."

She munched a last tuber and we hop-ran back to the village. The fact was, we couldn't see the sun—only feel it. Some of the groups further off were already worshiping the sensation as God's touch, I'd heard. Natural enough.

But the sun's rays were necessary for color refraction. At night it was sonar alone, a strange, eerie landscape of white outlines against pitch-black, which could be extremely deceiving. Best to be in a place you knew well after dark.

No lights or fires illuminated the town at night, but the familiar, simple surroundings were easy to manage with the sonar.

After the kids were asleep in their own rooms I sat down with George Haspinol again. It was the first time in several days we'd had the chance to talk; he was often out and around, telling his tales, teaching whom he could, trying to keep the frail threads which tied the local community together from becoming frayed.

"How'd it go?" I asked him.

"I'm winning a few small battles," he replied wearily, "but I'm losing the war. You know that. Guz, Gal, and Rum are proof of it. My own children speak like savages, and none of them can count past five. They go through the motions for the old man, but soon they'll be full-grown and leave to stake out their own houses in new places, have their own families, which will learn even less of the language and culture. I'm told that already the language just the other side of the hills is about eighty or so words, and so distorted you could hardly make it out. They're becoming the cows you talked about, Bar—by multiplication and geography alone."

I nodded. "But you know it's coming, the holocaust," I responded. "Even with the grass growing again almost overnight, and new tubers sprouting all the time, you're hoof-deep in feces out there, and just eating is a mob scene." I had done a narrow-pulse scan that day; on normal, or wide pulse, I could "see" only three or four hundred meters before the sound was too diffuse to return. Each of our pulses was distinctive, individualistic—even with thousands of people pulsing you always were sensitive to your own. On narrow, though, you shot your full wad at one spot—maybe only a few meters wide, but it carried for a couple of kilometers. I never ran out of Choz to count, nor could I count them all.

"The water's rising, there's signs the winter snows have melted at last," he said evenly. "Breeding season is only weeks away, maybe less. It may be the last one before the whole thing caves in."

I nodded, and shifted subjects. "George, you promised to explain this all to me. Who *they* are and what we're doing here."

He sighed, and stretched out.

"It's—well, you ran all sorts of tests before coming in, didn't you?"

"Sure," I replied. "More sophisticated than yours, I bet. And I found nothing."

"You didn't know what to look for. Did you find a virus, a tiny colony of sub-microorganisms that built honeycombs at a fast rate?"

"Yes," I told him. "Sure. They didn't affect the test animals, but that's why I came in with full suit and pack."

He shifted slightly. "That figures. They didn't do anything to our test animals, either—or, for that matter, us. We were extracautious, even had a small group living here for a couple of weeks before we committed the main colony. The things aren't much more than enzymes—simple protein molecules, apparently. The only effect they seemed to have was to replace many of the cellular enzymes. There was a slight narcotic effect at the beginning, and we wondered about it, but they were so firmly lodged that to kill them would be to kill the people. They didn't seem to do any harm, and, once they'd moved in, actually made the cells work better, not worse. So, after a while, we committed. Thanks to Fitzgerald we'd been subjectively aloft only a little over thirty years, and we'd limited reproduction in that time just in case the voyage would be a long one. This planet seemed heaven-sent, and so we committed."

"It's a simple virus, then?" I asked, incredulous. "But—all this is so *planned*."

"A whole new form of life," he replied. "It thinks—

make no mistake about it. What sort of thoughts, only God knows. Certainly too alien for us to understand. But thought? It got into us, and within days had mutated itself to adapt to our cellular structure. It fitted, it worked—and it bided its time, didn't do much else, except maybe a few favors. It repaired and replaced damaged cells fast, it made you more alert, healthier. What gets me is that it waited until we were all down, supplies, everything, before it struck. It started on everything first—except the shuttle. It left that alone, for some reason. When things started to fall apart, a couple of the colonists made it to the shuttle, managed to take off, made the *Peace Victory*. Without food to fuel the metabolic changes, the new organisms couldn't act, but the runaways were helpless. They needed a lot more people to run the ship, and most of the supplies they needed to live were now down here.

"Finally, near starvation, they decided to come back, for better or worse. It was that or starve. We'd all changed by that time, so I got to see what it looked like in others, and this time watched the creatures dissolve the ship with secretions of some kind."

"But why these shapes?" I mused. "Why not just take over people as they were?"

"Oh, some of it you can see right off," George replied. "First of all, we needed to be strictly herbivores so they could manage the food supply and we wouldn't louse up their ecosystem by killing the other animals. Tools and artifacts threaten the ecology, too, so you take away hands. Tough, dark skin for protection against the grasses and the sun. The ability to travel long distances, so we'd spread out fast."

"But why the strange optical system?" I asked.

"I don't know. My best guess is that it's multipurpose. The color code eliminates everything except what you have to know about to live and survive. Makes it harder to muck with the environment, makes it easy and convenient to live in it. Also, they can induce hormonal flows and guide them with color stimulus. You already experienced some of the things they could do when they forced you to stuff yourself during the Change. You'll see more during the breeding season. They are in every cell of your body, and as long as they understand the cellular function and its place in your scheme—which they designed—they can induce almost anything. As for the sonar—I suspect that the pulse and return is something they can easily convert to their own terms better than sight. After all, how many eyes does a virus have?"

I nodded. A logical reason for everything, I thought. Intelligent viruses—or, perhaps, a single organism with many parts. Surely one of them, even a colony, couldn't do this alone. There was almost certainly a reason for every component they'd built into us.

"George?" I said suddenly, a thought striking.

"Umh?" he responded sleepily.

"Anything that smart has to know how to count, doesn't it?"

"I suppose so," he mumbled.

"And we're breeding fast to breed the humanity out of us—but also to provide new hosts for the colonies of viruses, right?"

"Um hum," came the reply.

"George, they've *got* to know they're at the limits of their world's population."

Suddenly his head lifted a little. "Lord! You're right! And they're much too clever to let the situation really get out of hand. That means they have to allow death or no birth, *have* to!" There was new hope in his voice.

"I don't think so," I said, trying to think. "That would mean limiting their own expanding population. Now that they've got the means to do it, I don't think they'll want to stop. No, there's something else, something we're missing." Another thought struck me.

"They must know we're intelligent. They must know we think, reason. You know they could lobotomize us in a minute. They have something else up. Otherwise, why not just use their own animals? Why us?"

"I've often wondered about that," he replied. "I don't know the answer. I *do* know that they're fast approaching a break point—too many people, and the bulk of the people naturally and normally a planned creature of their own capable of reasoned intelligence but culturally animalistic."

"Then, if they can impose behavior, and if the average person considers this normal, what do we have?"

"Organic robots," George said in a curious tone. "A total merging of the two life forms with the virus in charge."

"But where does it go from there?" I wondered. There was no clear answer to that, and we could only lie there, awake, trying to figure it all out.

Six

Time flowed on, and I tended to fit into the routine existence of Patmos. It's funny, but the human mind is distinctive not only for its reasoning abilities, but also for its incredible adaptability.

Ship piloting, for example, is difficult to do. It's done by mental commands that must be instantaneous; life-or-death decisions must be made at all times, particularly in takeoffs, landings, and dockings. The first few weeks in pilot simulation I crashed repeatedly; I thought I would never get the idea of communicating complex instructions with mental nudges while watching sensor data and the like and interpreting them. Yet, within a month, I was not only doing all that fairly routinely, but holding conversations with fellow trainees and copilots at the same time.

Patmos was like that. Here I was, after thirty-six years as a human being, suddenly a four-legged hopping animal that saw by built-in sonar, and yet, by the fifth week doing so was as natural to me as if I had been born to it. Visions, appearances of other creatures that would have made me laugh or perhaps turn away, now seemed normal, even beautiful and sleek.

Our ability to adapt mentally to any situation is why we got to the stars, why the Choz were here at all. Even so, the population problem weighed heavily on me, along with the strong and unshakable suspicion that something a lot darker than the mere transformation of a group of people into a new and alien culture was at stake.

Note that "mere"—indeed! How quickly one adapts!

When George's companion, Joanna, returned with the other three of the last brood from an extended visit to some of her children from the past cycle, I was crowded out of even the large leader's quarters. The time had come to do some poking about anyway, I thought, and so I left them and decided on a trip over the hills to see what the situation was further afield.

Following the river's course up to its source was tricky. Less vegetation of the edible kind could be found as you went up, and the plant growth rate seemed slower, more normal, than down on the plains. This area looked more and more as if it were the way the planet might have been before the virus inside us decided to change all that.

As for people—Choz, that is—there were few, and soon none at all. The air was chillier, too, the temperature dropping about a degree per three-hundred meters. The hills weren't tall, really, but the valleys were deep and sheltered, some much colder than the surrounding hillsides or the plains—as much as a twenty-five-degree temperature drop in places the sun never saw.

The virus didn't like the cold, I discovered. Cold places had a menacing pale yellow, the danger color, even when sonar showed no threat other than the chill, which penetrated a bit into my thick, hairy hide.

When I persisted in going through such places despite the color warnings, the virus tried getting tougher. I fought it off with difficulty. It was easier knowfortable, feverish at times. When that didn't stop me the virus tried triggering the hunger mechanism, but I fought it off with difficulty. It was easier knowing what was causing these things; the intellect wasn't supreme, but it did help fight the impulses—helped me more than most, since what I resented more than anything was the fact that such reactions were being *imposed*.

Seiglein Corporation imposed. Its will was law; its people were its property, possessions just like the buildings and the power plants and the ships with which it controlled the trade between hundreds of planets. Scouts were the only semifree spirits left in Seiglein's universe; that was the heart of why we were out there, the hundreds of men and women who couldn't stand taking orders.

This is why I could fight the virus. Every once in a while they'd hit on something that would work, turn me, make me do their bidding, but the same thing didn't work twice. They controlled the cells, the body fluids and functions, but they could not control the mind directly without destroying it.

It took four days to get across the hills, days of loneliness that were, for me, very satisfying ones as I proved to myself that I was not anybody's property, that I could still be me in this crazy world.

From a ledge on the other side of the hills I could narrow-pulse for great distances. There were rolling hills on this side, more trees, a network of larger and more imposing rivers. Food-color was all over, and I was hungry after the sparse diet of mountain grasses.

As for Choz, they were present. I made out the slight silver of at least eight towns too far to pulse, showing up only as tiny blobs of the web-color to my vision.

Gingerly I made my way down the last slopes and joined the large herd grazing all around. There weren't quite as many as I'd first calculated there would be, and as I ate I considered this. True, I had seen only a small section of this place as yet, but there should be more according to my math.

As dusk approached, invisible to me except for the gradual fading of the colors, I headed for the nearest town, hoping at least to find members of the original party, like George, or near-generation to those pioneers.

As I hopped into the town—quite a bit larger than the point—a young female came up to me.

"Hi wudja pop?" she asked.

"Huh?" I responded. "I don't understand."

"Wudja pop?" she repeated, getting a little annoyed. I could only shake my head and try again.

"I don't understand you," I said slowly and carefully. "Are there any Firsts or Seconds here?" This meant old-timers, first or second generation.

She caught a little of it. "Fusts nap," she responded in what was an obvious negative. "Secs Mara dere." She gestured with her tail to a spot down the street, but it was impossible to tell where.

I thanked her, though she probably didn't understand anything but the implied sentiment, and continued on down the street.

The town was getting crowded as the mob retreated to their homes for the night. They all seemed to speak variations of the gibberish the girl was spouting, and I could make nothing out of it.

I seemed to remember some teacher saying that the faster a species breeds and matures the more it mutates. Well, there was only one physical mutation here, but the sociocultural mutation was obviously in full swing. The youngest generations were speaking a completely different language even this soon and this close; I was fairly certain that it would get more diffuse, more alien, the farther away I roamed from the home of a First like George.

There was a large building at the end of the street, similar to the one at the point, although there was no sign of a church. I decided that this must house the ranking member of the tribe and went up to it, poked my head in the doorway, and asked, "Anybody here understand what I'm saying?"

There was a rustle, and I could sound three or four almost grown younglings, one of whom said, "Wudja yerring ja?" in a decidedly nasty tone—a young male, just starting to feel his strength.

Suddenly a girl's voice said sharply, "Layrf, Mag!" and she came to the door.

"I'm sorry," she said. "It's been a long time since we've heard straight speech around here."

"Things are certainly different," I replied apologetically. "I'm Bar Holliday, from the point."

There was still enough light to note her radiate some surprise.

"Holliday! You're the new one, then. The scout pilot!"

"News travels fast."

She shrugged. "News travels fast anywhere, although it gets somewhat distorted by the time it gets to us. Come! You can share my room for the night and tell me everything!"

We went to the rear of the building, an extremely well-constructed one with at least eight spacious compartments, and I stretched out tiredly on a very thick mat of soft, broad leaves that were much more comfortable than anything I'd experienced at the point. And, of course, for the past few days I'd been sleeping on rocks and grass, in the open.

"I sound you need a preen," she said, and I grunted. "I've been across the mountains, out of touch for days," I told her.

She proceeded to do the preen, which was needed much more than I'd suspected. Saliva salve or not, some of the burrs and little insects were deeply imbedded and hurt like hell.

Finished, she reclined on the mat and faced me.

"Well, I guess we should start by completing the introductions," she laughed. "Now that I've chewed you to pieces and all. I'm Mara, Second Mother to Gar-town here."

I thought for a moment. A Second, the first I'd really run into. Seconds, George had said, were taught intensively by their parents and were in many ways human-culture, yet it was one generation removed. They knew all the stories, the legends, and had as

50

much knowledge as could be passed on to them, yet their only experience was of being Choz. She has never seen the sky or the countless stars, I thought, nor held anything in her hands, yet superficially she was as culturally similar to me as George.

"Tell me all about yourself," she urged.

I chuckled. "Not much to tell, really. We licked the problem of faster-than-light travel just a few years after the *Peace Victory* was launched, and I've been on the job the last several years discovering new worlds for humanity to breed into."

She sighed, and I could tell she was romanticizing.

"To go such distances—I've never been further than from here to the point myself, where I was born. I've been here I don't know how long—a dozen or more melts, anyway." She shifted slightly. "Tell me—what do they look like, these stars?"

I reached for an analogy. "You know how water sparkles as it flows?" I tried, and she nodded. "Imagine just the sparkles, millions of them, against a field of jet black, and you'll get some idea."

She tried but couldn't manage it.

"The people who live out there—are they happier than we? Better off?" she asked, reminding me of Guz's question.

There was still only one answer. "I don't know," I replied. "Here all things are provided us and we are managed by an unseen intelligence. Out there it's pretty much the same, only the intelligence lives in a great city on a planet that is almost all city, and everybody knows who and what it is."

We talked for most of the evening, she full of questions about things she could only imagine but never comprehend fully—a deaf person can academically grasp the concept of music, but never experience it—thrilled to have somebody exotic to talk to. That she was a bored woman was obvious.

"It's the breed," she explained. "Each generation is more than the last, and outnumbers the last. You can't teach or minister to them in just the short time we have. My own children are so different that I can hardly relate to them anymore. The old ways, the old beliefs, are going as we get more and more removed from our Firsts."

I nodded. "I don't know what is being created here, but it will be a different kind of person, surely, than you and I can know or understand. Old George talked about it at the point a lot."

"George!" she exclaimed. "I should like to see him again. It has been so long, so very long. Tell me, how is he?"

"Good, but kind of down in spirit, like you."

"Yes, well, he is my father, you know. It's natural I should miss him."

Sure he was, I thought, feeling stupid. If the others spread out as much as possible, and she came from the point, odds were good she was one of George's first brood. "You ought to get back to see him," I suggested. "I'm sure he'd like that."

Her voice seemed strained, emotionally clouded, as she said, "I—well, there's always children to see to, and I couldn't see him without them."

For a moment I didn't understand, and said as much.

"Well, ah, oh—it's so very *hard* to know how to say it. Father and the others, they were a Christian group, you know. You've never been through the Breed. There's no choice, no thinking there. When it came on the second time, well, George was First Male and strongest. My children are his children and his grandchildren. It's normal here—but he couldn't handle it. It was against his beliefs."

So that was it, I thought sadly. So much for acculturation. Incest was still a potent taboo, and George had committed it, was afraid he'd do it again—probably *had* done it again. She'd inherited some of the meaningless, in the context of the Choz, revulsion that her father and the other Firsts had felt.

"That just proves how much we cause our own problems, and other's," I comforted. "After all, in a human context inbreeding causes problems. Some, anyway. But not here, not among the Choz."

Where was that aptitude for mental adaptation now? I wondered. Some things were too deeply ingrained in certain people for their own good. A lot of misery had been caused in this way.

"You still should go," I urged. "Why not come back with me? It looks like the kids in there can take care of themselves."

"Maybe," she replied. "We'll see."

I stayed maybe a week, maybe more, in the town. Mara was good company; always inquisitive, always wanting to hear stories about my exploits, which I was never at a loss for. She had several sessions a day with different younglings, trying to teach them what she could, but it was a hopeless battle. Few stayed long to hear her, and those that did were only mildly curious.

I could take no part in these sessions. The language had changed too much. With each lesson she seemed to become a little more despondent, and a little more receptive to suggestions to something different, breaking free of the mold.

I liked her for that. She had a quick wit and an insatiable curiosity combined with a naïveté that allowed her to accept my boastful stories uncritically.

But, most important, she was frustrated with this dull and boring life, which was amazing because, unlike me, she'd known nothing else and didn't quite understand what she craved.

On my tours I also discovered that even though most of the last brood looked adult, they were really of different ages. The Breed came upon people at different times although at regular intervals.

The next session of the Breed—after the interregnum that occurred only once for a short period every two years—was coming fast upon us. Some of the females were growing sleeker, their color and texture brightening and heightening, and I could feel strange stirrings within myself as well. I had landed, it appeared, near the end of one cycle, and now I was about to go into my first.

The change was as apparent in Mara as in anyone. It was an indefinable emotional twinge inside. Oddly, the women seemed aware of it only indirectly, by observing the reactions of the males. Not all of them turned me on, just a small percentage. If one male had to service five or more females, it couldn't be done in one cycle, which explained why there seemed less population pressure than reason had dictated. That did not alter the fact that this world was headed for collapse, only delayed it a few years.

"Let's go visit George," I urged her one day. "Come on."

"But—The Breed!" she protested. "It'll take a week or more to cut south to the pass."

"*Over* the mountains, the way I came in, not around and through."

She nervously scanned the hills.

"I don't know," she began hesitantly.

"C'mon!" I urged. "You're bored and frustrated here. You know it. This is a new experience, an adventure, something different! Come with me. I know he'd love to see you!"

Finally she relented. "I'll do it," she decided. "When do we go?"

"How about tomorrow morning?" I responded.

I dreamed for the first time that night. It was funny —I almost never dreamed, and hadn't yet done so here. Of course, I probably had, but I never remembered any of them, which amounts to the same thing.

This particular dream was one of those weird ones you can never quite figure out, but it was filled with the color green and with strange feelings, urges, and impulses. Superimposed over it all seemed to be a bright violet netting, like a honeycomb, active, growing, reaching out, building, doing things. I seemed to run in and out of the violet netting, which grew around me, trying to trap me against that green field, yet there were roughly rectangular holes through which I could crawl and escape.

I awoke suddenly, feeling funny, as if my mouth were full of mush. I scanned the room. Mara was still sleeping, snoring slightly, and all was still and quiet. I bit down, seeming to snap something spongy as I did so. I scanned the area ahead of my face and found, to my surprise, that I had for the first time secreted webbing from the flap in my tongue and had somehow constructed a tiny web-wall, now hardening. I could feel the stuff in the canal in my tongue, like a piece of chalk or stick yet still soft and flexible.

I lay there for some time trying to make sense out of what was happening to me, before drifting off into a light and uncomfortable sleep.

The next morning I apologized to Mara for the mess. I'd built a low barrier between us, it seemed. She laughed, made a joke about my true feelings coming out in my dreams, then explained to me that it was a common thing and easily corrected, if a bit messy and hard to clean up.

The webbing dissolved in urine.

That concept wasn't something I would ever think of, yet it opened up a possibility in my mind that was exciting: liberating my ship. I had gone out to that field every day and seen that mound of webbing locking it in. The ship was still in there, all right—I felt sure of it. I don't know why; it should have been broken down with the rest of the artifacts. Instead, it had been covered, shielded, and protected.

Two or three minutes, that's all I would need. Two or three minutes and I could lift off, even without hands.

Then I recalled George's mentioning that a couple of the early colonists had made it off the planet in their shuttle. But they had been doomed anyway, of course, since they couldn't get anywhere in the shuttle and the big ship was beyond their management. Yet the shuttle had been destroyed only after it proved a threat. The virus hadn't been able to eat it away in the time it took to take off, and space had killed the virus clinging to the outer shell.

Why had the virus been so ineffective?

The armor, probably. Spacecraft were made of the toughest materials, not like the simple suits, prefabs, and the like you'd normally use.

But I didn't have a shuttle; I had a small FTL ship that could be run not by mechanical controls but by direct impulse from the brain.

Now I was more anxious than ever to get back.

Seven

The trip back was easier than the trip up. We had each other to help over the rough spots. The bugs still didn't like those cold places, but with me there urging her on, egging her on, Mara proved to be as stubborn and determined as I.

As we made our way, both of us began changing. I could feel it, knew that it was she who was changing and I who was reacting. Yet once the burning started, it would not go away. Her green seemed to get brighter as I watched, becoming more and more intense; her awkward Choz body seemed to grow beautiful, sleek, attractive, her every move a thing of beauty. And there was the scent—a smell that was subtle at the start, but growing more and more powerful, more alluring, as time passed.

It was the Breed, I knew. I'd seen animals react strangely when the females were in heat, and this is what I was now experiencing firsthand.

"What am I going to do about it?" I asked her plaintively. Until this started I had experienced no sexual urges whatsoever, no attraction beyond a platonic liking for another person.

"The Breed is normal and natural," she replied soothingly. "I counted on this in deciding to come. We will mate and breed before we reach the point and this will ease the problem with Father."

Stupid me, I thought sourly. Being in space so long cuts you off from the practical. Still, I didn't understand why her calculating response bothered me—I had certainly enjoyed sex with many women I'd hardly known, and this wasn't much different. Better, really, since the act was such a natural and normal part of life on this world, particularly *her* whole life, that I should have just taken it in stride as I had the rest of this strange experience.

Maybe I was overreacting because of the way all this was being done—from outside, by automatic stimulus, imposed again. That antiauthority response again. Or, maybe it was just fear of not knowing what to do, or what was to be done. I would have to depend on her for that.

We were on the river course down to the point, less than a day from our goal. Mara had puzzled over why nothing had happened yet, the buildup being slower than the normal pattern. On this world *everything* happened according to the normal pattern.

But now, today, this moment, the waiting was over.

I didn't have to worry about how to do anything; everything was all done for me. She was suddenly a blazing green, overpowering, as was her maddening scent. I couldn't think of anything else, see anything else. I sent out a pulse to her and she stopped. Suddenly I was locked on; the normal pulsing became a steady, overpowering scream directly at her, full force. She stood there, frozen by it, as if hypnotized.

I moved close to her, swaying the sonic beam back and forth rhythmically, and she swayed to my tune and direction, expression blank, as if in some sort of trance. I forced the beam upward, up again, stroking her with sound, and she rose, leaning back on her massive tail, leaning, leaning further back than I had ever seen any Choz go, almost completely doubled back, so that her circular vaginal cavity was exposed.

Then I moved to within a meter of her and stood on my tail as well. I could feel my own breathing, heavy, rhythmic, and a tiny corner of my mind noted that her breathing was in perfect time to my own. Everything was a complete blur, a rush of urge and emotion, both of us in some sort of orgasmic fog.

Suddenly she sent out a steady pulse to me, stronger, stronger, until her far-different frequency and my own were in almost perfect tune. I edged close to her, following the beam linking the two pairs of horns, and then we were locked, linked together in that eerie tableau for who knew how long.

When, finally, that part was over, the whole process was not. Slowly we moved in perfect unison, bringing our bodies back up, then forward. Her two horns touched my curled ones, fitted through the loops in mine.

The sensation felt like an overpowering electric shock. We linked in some way, became as one, moved as one, saw as one, felt as one. I was both bodies and she was both bodies, yet there was no thought, no consciousness beyond the overpowering feelings.

Slowly she withdrew, and we turned and stood side by side as one organism. We moved to a clearing near the river and, together, we spun a house. It was beautiful, intricate, and came from someplace other than our minds, since I had no way of knowing how to do this on my own.

When we finished we lined the floor with leaves and grass, and went inside. She lay on the floor, on her back, a position that was extremely unnatural to a Choz under other circumstances, and I placed myself over her, penetrated again, and settled down atop her. We maintained this position, unmoving, unthinking, for what must have been days—I later learned that it had been ten days!—without thought, without any sensation but the overpowering one. Finally, I felt a touch, and drew back, back, so that I stood not over her but in front of her. Suddenly, in front of me, the first egg emerged, a flashing, almost blinding white and quite large. Then came a second, and then a third.

I waited, but no more came. She sat up, and the

fold or flap on her marsupial pouch seemed creased, part open.

I reached out with a forehoof, placed it over the first egg, the three-part cleft opening just exactly wide enough to go around the top half of the egg, and I lifted it slowly and carefully placed it in her pouch, then the second.

Then the ritual was reversed, and I leaned back, opening my pouch. Whereupon she leaned forward, grasped the third egg, and placed it in my pouch. We both were lying on our backs, cradled on our own bushy tails.

Exhausted, for the first time in ten days we both slept.

Eight

Mara was just coming in when I awoke. Her color was neutral green once again, and all the sensations of the past ten days were a dim and blurry memory.

I felt weak as I got to my feet, and a little dizzy. She saw me and stopped.

"How are you feeling?" she asked, concerned.

"Terrible," I responded. "My God! Do we go through that every two years?"

"No," she said slowly. "*I* go through it once every two years. You—well, as often as every two months until the next in-between time."

It made me ill to think about that. Males *would* be studs in this system; we'd have to average one every three and a half months or so.

"Why do I have an egg in my pouch?" I asked. I could barely feel it there, but I was nonetheless conscious of it.

She laughed. "The eggs are neuter. The sex of the child is determined by its hatch-place. In a few days they will hatch, and attach to the inner wall of the skin. That way they will be fed, and with the nourishment will come the instructions on sexual development. No one knows how—we have no way of knowing here."

"I—" I began, then almost collapsed.

She came over to me, radiating concern. "Here! Come outside and eat. You have had nothing for a long time and are very weak. After you'll feel a little sick as I do now, but that is normal. Then, only then, will we talk about the strangeness."

I managed to stumble outside. The food-color was overwhelming and I started in. It wasn't the ravenous hunger of the changing; in fact, I ate a little, then stopped, then managed a little more. The sensation was more like one of starvation, where everything looks wonderful but you feel sick when you face the food about which you dream. It took me about three hours, and I still didn't feel right, but I was convinced that I could manage no more. I went back to the hut, still feeling weak, as she had warned, and sour as well.

Even so, I took time to study the house. We had built it together in the Breed, yet I still couldn't have done anything so elaborate on my own. Everything was so much of a blur I had only vague memories of its construction, but I admired the work.

She heard me approach, and came out of the house.

"That's amazing!" I exclaimed to her. "The house, I mean. Did I—did *we* build that? Did we really build that?"

She nodded. "If there is no house of your mate's own webbing, one will be built. This is only the third time for me, but it's as good as any of them."

I agreed. Still feeling lousy, I lay down on the grass near the house and stretched out as best I could. No position felt comfortable, but it was better than nothing.

"You'll get used to it," Mara said, coming over and lying down near me.

And this, too, was strange, I thought. The whole thing—why it disturbed me so. It was wholly animalistic, instinctive. There was nothing of one's will involved, nor of one's true emotions, either. There was no romance, no love, not even the sense of fulfilling a need to combat loneliness that would make somebody use a prostitute. No, the whole process was totally without any inkling of humanity, and that's what bothered me the most.

I had to get the hell off this planet, or die. Not being suicidal, I would still prefer death to my current situation—and I marveled at how the older ones, the Firsts at least, could feel other than this way as well. But these were ordinary people, for the most part, I realized. Like those of my own world. All their needs serviced, on the social dole. Even those who protested wanted only a world more utopian, more perfect. They didn't have my needs, my fierce belief that only in struggle was man something more than the animals.

Modern humanity might as well be these docile animals, I knew. This is what the reformers wanted, lacking only population control. A world without worries over food, over war, over jealousy and hatred. A world without care or caring of any kind, including the caring of one person for another.

A world where thinking was also unnecessary, obsolete.

"What are you thinking about?" Mara asked, concerned. "Your aura shows great disturbance."

"Just thinking," I replied. "And that's something you shouldn't do on this world. There's no room for it."

"And is that true on your world?" she asked.

I sighed. "Not anymore. Not really. Those of us who do think are either fitted into the corporate mold or put in jobs like mine, where they're segregated from society even as they serve it."

"I think I understand," Mara replied. "I often think about what my father taught me. The colonists were pioneers, too, you know. They wanted to poke into places nobody else had been, and to solve the problem of setting up a new society on a new world. They—the Firsts, I mean—always felt cheated that they hadn't the chance to do that."

I nodded. My stomach felt a little better, but I was still light-headed.

"I can't understand why the virus lets us keep thinking. They've already demonstrated they can stop that, by cutting through a part of our brain. Why leave us as fully self-aware individuals at all?"

She shrugged. "Who knows what such creatures

think, or how they think? How could we ever even contact them, or they us? What do we have in common? And what can we do about this life, anyway?"

Those were indeed the questions that begged answering. Of the first, I could only guess. They *knew* we were intelligent, knew even how to cut that intelligence off. They knew quite a lot about us. I suspected that they lived their own lives through us, saw what we saw, felt what we felt. I suspected that was the reason for the weird vision; this was the method by which they, as well as we, could see. Optic nerves to neural impulses to the brain would not be enough. They could neither interpret the signals nor get into the brain to have them interpreted.

But sound—you *felt* sound. It was vibration, air movement. This could go to several sources.

"It was a strange Breed," Mara said suddenly.

"Huh?" I managed, breaking off my reverie.

"Only three eggs. That has never happened before. It's always six."

"Our masters are smart," I told her. "They can count. They see that we're breeding ourselves into a situation where there won't be enough food for all. I suspect this is but the first stage of a complex change— that they will eventually stop the Breed entirely, or stretch it out, or introduce death by aging. It's either that or some must starve."

But was that the only possibility? I mused. Was it, indeed? They reproduced through us; we'd been the means of greatly expanding their race. Could they give that up now?

They'd have to, I told myself. There was no other way. They must have had to do it before, with the animals here.

Suddenly I felt a shock run through me. The animals! They were a normal population! If these creatures could breed any living matter into anything else and set the rules for the organism, why hadn't they done it to the others? This world was too normal, too

64

ordinary except for the Choz. That revelation had been what had been bothering me all along.

The virus could not possibly have existed on this world much longer than humanity. Nor, in fact, could it have evolved here—the kinds of pressures that would cause such an intelligence to evolve just couldn't be found here.

The more I thought about it, the more I wondered.

That virus could not exist!

This world, the Choz, this system, could not exist!

Not without violating everything we know about evolution.

"Mara!" I almost yelled at her. "I think I've just discovered something!"

"What are you talking about?" she responded, not sure of my sanity. Truthfully, neither was I.

"The only way—the *only* way that virus could possibly exist on this planet is if it came here with us!" I blurted. "It's as alien to this place as we are. And if I could get to those tapes in the *Peace Victory* I think I can prove it."

I became extremely excited though I couldn't put my finger on the why of it. Somehow, I felt, I was nearing the solution, and only a few more pieces of the puzzle would be needed to get everything straight.

Mara seemed less interested; although bored by this world and amused by my emotional outbursts, she was unable to see the import of them.

I was convinced that another conversation with George would put the last pieces into place, and I was, therefore, anxious to be off. Since Mara had helped in the building of the first unit of George's great house, she could be as comfortable there when the young came as in the little place we'd built.

Oddly, she was reluctant to leave, and it was some time before I realized why. First, she was still extremely nervous at seeing her father after all these years, and even more unsure as to how she would be received. Second, the isolated up-valley spot was her first real rest away from people and the responsibility her being a Second entailed. Returning to the mass of bodies below would bring back all the pressures. And, finally, there was me.

Not that I was a charming rascal and she was madly in love with me. I doubt if someone not a First could conceive of real love for another, unrelated individual. But, I was different—I talked different, felt different, acted different from anybody she'd ever known, Firsts included. Even the Firsts had been ideologues; I remembered George's telling me that some of the Firsts thought this really *was* paradise and that all of the changes and the like were God's will. I was the first rebel on this world, the first person who refused to accept with stoic fatalism what sort of a life was offered.

Finally, I talked her into moving on, and we made our way down the mountain the additional half a day's journey to the point. It looked just as when I'd left it, of course. There were a lot more houses out on the plain; another village was building after the last Breed, clearly.

George wasn't in, but I saw Guz, still not at puberty but very close if her color was any indication. She told me that George was at his favorite spot on the plain near the river. The Breed was always hard on George, and he was often antisocial for weeks afterward.

Good Christians just aren't made for incestuous harems.

We splashed through the shallow river and down the far bank, but, as we approached George's spot under the shade of some spreading palmlike trees, Mara slowed and stopped.

"What's the matter?" I called, coming to a halt and whirling in one motion. I was getting pretty good at being a four-footed hopping animal.

"I—I think you'd better go on," she said hesitantly. "I'll join you—later. After . . ."

66

Her voice trailed off, but I could see her problem.

"Don't worry about it so much!" I chided, then softened my tone. "Look, you wait here, relax, graze. I'll prepare the way."

This settled, it still took me a while to find George.

I could tell by his richer blue that he was with egg himself, and through the color came an aura that cried despondency. Even so, he looked up as I approached and seemed to brighten as he recognized me.

"Bar Holliday!" he called cheerfully. "Well! You made it over and back, eh?"

"That I did, George," I responded lightly. "Not a long or a hard trip, but one with some new discoveries and experiences."

His tone darkened with his hue. "You experienced the Breed, then."

I nodded. "That's some crazy way of reproducing. There must be a reason for it, but I can't think of what."

"Probably takes that long to transfer the viral strain within the egg," he said in that clinical tone he sometimes adopted.

I thought for a minute. Yes, that somehow seemed to make sense. Ten days—anything could happen in ten days considering that it had taken barely three to reshape me. Something definitely went on during that period—not for the mating couple, certainly. For the tiny masters within.

"George, I think I'm close to the solution of this crazy mess," I told him.

He looked startled by the comment. "Eh? You mean the population thing? They seem to have solved that— three eggs this time."

"No, no, not that. The whole puzzle. Look, it suddenly came to me after the Breed that this whole thing is nonsense. It makes no sense at all. The world is too illogical, just as *we* are illogical. Let me ask you—was there any disease during the voyage of the *Peace Victory?*"

He frowned, remembering. "Why, yes, there was, come to think of it. Some sort of intestinal problem. Had a hell of a time locating it and producing a serum."

I smiled broadly, knowing the answer to my question as I asked it. "It was a virus, wasn't it, George?"

He looked puzzled. "Why, yes, come to think of it, it was. Hard to remember these things—it happened so long ago." He stopped suddenly, seeing where the conversation was going.

"Oh, no," he protested. "No, it wasn't anything like *our* virus. Not at all."

"I think it was," I persisted. "No, not the form we have now, but an earlier strain. You know there's always been trouble with viruses in spaceflight—they reproduce so incredibly fast that minor forces, radiation and the like, can produce mutations that would normally take millions of years to develop."

"Not possible, though," he insisted. "We licked it. We analyzed some of the victims at the onset, fed the cultures into the computer, and out came the serum that effectively eliminated the virus."

So there it was. The last link. Just a couple of more pieces and everything would fit.

"That ship's computer of yours—it's an antique by my standards. I couldn't even figure out how to turn it on. Tell me, George—was it self-aware? Did you have self-aware comps in those days?"

"Why sure it was," the older man replied with pride. "Best machine built up to its time. A whole new breed. We called it Moses, because it was leading us to the promised land."

There was the last piece. I now knew where the virus had come from, why it was here and why it had done what it had done. I even had a fairly good idea what it was up to now. The only remaining question was what I would do with this information. If I was right, I was close to developing the worst case of paranoia that anyone ever had.

Somehow this brought Mara to mind. I'd totally forgotten her.

"George," I said softly. "Mara's here."

His head came up like a shot, and he was suddenly tense. Then, very gradually, he seemed to soften, melt before me.

"Mara," he sighed, both sad and wistful.

"She mated with me on the way here," I told him. "She wants to see you badly. She's been so lonely over with the ignorant younglings."

"Mara," he repeated, his aura almost misting. I tried to imagine what was going through his mind, but could not.

"Do you want to see her?" I asked softly.

He seemed to regain control of himself. He straightened, became more solid, dignified.

"Why, yes, of course I do. Where—where is she?"

"Not far," I told him. "Wait here—I'll get her. And, remember it's as hard on her as on you."

As I walked back I reflected how odd it was that great things should seem small and small things greatly magnified when seen on a personal level.

I brought Mara to him, slowly, hesitantly. She was shy, uncertain, nervous, and in the Choz culture all of this showed.

They stood there, just looking at each other for the longest time, until, finally, he approached her, a riot of emotional hues, and rubbed against her tenderly.

I left, satisfied that that part of my mission was now complete.

As for me, I now had the puzzle solved but not my course of action. What I did have, for the first time, were choices, options, ways to go.

Slowly I approached the mound of silver webbing, a small hill on the plain. My ship—my ship was in there, perfectly preserved, still on, still functioning.

I knew that in a way the little masters of this

world could not know. I knew it because technology does not stand still. I knew it because the computer that ran and guided my ship was not a self-aware machine like that of the *Peace Victory,* but a part of myself. I could feel it, sense it as I grew closer.

In there, too, I lived, awaiting the arrival of the body so that I could take off. It would not desert me as long as it knew I lived, but we could not make true contact until I was inside, no longer cut off from the mechanical link provided in my suit pack. I stood there, knowing now who had encased the ship so, and why, and wondered what to do.

I glanced around the plain on spray beam at the thousands of Choz quietly grazing, many talking in the short-speech, others curiously silent. They were watching me, I knew. All watching me. Wondering if this was the time. Wondering what I would do even as I pondered the same thing—not knowing, of course, that I knew.

I need George, I thought, my mind racing. I need George with me in the ship. Just George and me, alone. Once inside, once off-planet, we could talk of what had to be done, do what had to be done, face the enemy down once and for all.

Slowly, deliberately, I started back for the point.

Nine

For the next couple of days I let George be happy—
and he *was* happy. Mara meant more to him than
anything in this crazy world, and she clearly needed
him as well.

Each day I'd go back out to the plain, alone, to
graze near the ship and stare at it, sometimes for
hours. Often Guz would try and join me. It was a
natural response. I must be driving her crazy, I
thought; she was watching me, not knowing what I
was thinking or doing. I shooed her off each time.

Finally when I could stand it no longer, I spent a
great deal of time maneuvering George into an isolated area where none were nearby. I did this on
the pretense of showing him some interesting things
about the upper valley I'd noticed on the way down.
When we were far enough away from the point so
that I could scatter-beam no Choz, I stopped him.

"George, I lied to you," I told him, unashamed.
"There's nothing really new up here, no artifact."

"What's this all about, then?" he responded, curious.

"Everything, George, everything. Look, with a little
imagination and a lot of reasoning, I think I can
describe what this whole world's about. You stop me
and tell me when I'm wrong.

"It starts," I began, "with a group called the Communards, a back-to-the-land movement based on
Christianity and simple virtues, which attracted some
people with money and some, like yourself, who were

71

a part of the technocracy, who realized how dehumanizing things were becoming. You decided, along with others, that only a return to basics, a new start, on a far world not polluted by our plastic civilization, where the children and grandchildren would have to build a new world with their own sweat and labor while being raised on basic, old-fashioned, down-to-earth philosophy untainted by our socialist order and corporate syndicalism, would save man from becoming less than the machines that served him, a vegetable in a velvet-lined cage."

He nodded, a half-smile on his face, but said nothing.

"So you got together, sold everything you had, and built and outfitted the *Peace Victory*. It had what you needed, the latest in technology to carry you to your new home. But you didn't see, didn't realize, that you carried with you a disease that was at the heart of everything you despised in humanity. You were raised with it, and on it, as I was, and even rebelling against it you took it for granted, and you became a carrier."

"You don't mean the virus," he cut in, somewhat disbelieving.

"A virus, yes," I replied, "but not yet the one that now rules us. It's ancestor.

"Technocracy itself! Escaping from it, you lived in it, depended on it. You had the latest in self-aware artificial intelligence to make sure your air was pure, course was steady, food was produced. It even ministered to you when it was sick. You personalized it, made it part of your own cause in its programming. You called it Moses because it was to lead you to the promised land. But you forgot one thing about Moses, something I didn't know until I talked about your beliefs with Mara. That was the essence of why you didn't realize all this yourself, years ago. You were too close to the problem."

George sniffed a little derisively. "So what is all this leading to? If you've talked to Mara, you know the real Moses did indeed lead his people to the promised land."

"Oh, yes he did," I responded. "But there's a footnote to that event. He, himself, wasn't permitted to enter. Just like *your* Moses."

The truth hit him suddenly, with full force. "Oh! Jesus God!" was all he could manage.

"Moses was programmed to be one of you. He was your leader, your guide, your protector. He believed in his role implicitly. But, knowing the end, knowing *his* end, he felt cheated. Unlike your Biblical Moses, he'd done nothing to incur God's displeasure, nothing to deserve dying at the mountains, looking down on the promised land but unable to enter, ever. Doomed forever to look down, never to join in, never to reach the place so tantalizingly close, perhaps even to be turned off, killed, for doing his duty as God and his people had assigned him."

George was almost shaking. "Oh, Lord God! That virus—that simple, little intestinal virus. Moses mutated it, adapted it, created the alien strain we now have."

"Was Moses deactivated?" I asked him carefully.

His head, drooping a bit, shot up. "I don't know!" he almost screamed. "I assumed—but, well, that wasn't my responsibility."

"He did what he was told to do, gave you just what you said you wanted, although with machine logic. To a machine, a being who is a truly alien entity with our knowledge, your description of Eden, of true communism and Christian fulfillment, would be a herd of immortal deer in a world with plenty of food and no carnivores."

Least common denominator, I thought sadly. A mathematic concept. Boil down every utopia and you get that LCD—reduce man to the level of the herd animal without strife, fear, hostility, or death.

Only boredom.

"But why these forms?" George asked, voice cracking somewhat. "Why the Choz? Why the enormous reproduction rate?"

"What's a computer, anyway, George?" I asked, and not waiting for an answer, continued. "It's an artificial man-built brain. Yours is in the ship itself. It can't ever come down. But it can keep contact through our own senses. We see by reflected sound waves. Want to bet that the *Peace Victory*'s communication system picks up just about everything? Maybe, despite my precautions—this ledge here, our isolation—this conversation?"

The implications of what I was saying hit him. "Yes, yes! It might at that. So it sees what we see, hears what we hear, lives its own material life—many, many lives—through us. And—" he had it all now, "perhaps it also *transmits?*"

I nodded. "All of them—every one except the Firsts, which it is sworn to protect and comfort and listen to—are an extension of Moses. Not only did Moses enter the promised land, he *became* the promised land. And, because he interpreted the scripture and the goals of the group in his own, nonhuman, machine-oriented way, and because, as a ship's computer he has infinite patience, it's enough."

"Mara—" George said hesitantly. "Her, too?"

"Oh, yes," I replied, probably not as gently as I could. "Oh, that doesn't mean you've been talking to Moses the last few days. No, you've been talking to Mara, and Moses, if he chose, was experiencing everything she was."

"But this puts a lie to whatever positive I can find in this world!" he wailed. "*Damn* him! *Damn him to hell!*"

It was the first time I'd heard anyone curse on this

world, and the most vehemence I had ever seen over anything. If nothing else, I had introduced hatred on this world, hatred and revulsion.

Finally, he recovered, and looked at me, almost pleadingly. "Now what do we do?"

I sighed.

"He's finally reached the point where he can go no further on this world. He's not very creative—stealing bits and pieces of us from the native animals he himself surveyed and analyzed. At the start he made a lot of mistakes. The early first-stage incest, for example. The escape of the colonists by shuttle. How he must have feared they were on to him, were coming to shut him down! But he played dead, and they finally gave in. To seal everyone in, he destroyed the shuttle. He's got some slight flaws, you see. He's playing God, all right, but he's not omnipotent. He makes mistakes." I paused for a second, thinking of how to explain what was ahead.

"I think he's reached the turning point of social engineering on this world. He's most of the world, now, and he's stabilizing the population. Through his contact with the virus, he can program just about everybody except perhaps the Firsts. Probably intends a heavenly host eternally praying and glorifying God, the end vision of the book.

"Now it's time to spread the holy attainment."

George was aghast. "But—how?" he asked.

"Through me. My little ship can reach the *Peace Victory*. A small colony there will be easily nurtured. We can spread, invade other worlds, use the same techniques on a grander scale. He's going to be a missionary who can deliver, George, but he needs my ship."

The older man stood, deep in thought. Finally, he asked, "Can he get it? Can he use it?"

I shook my head negatively. "No, it's a different animal, so to speak. I'm sure he tried when I first boarded the *Victory* and found it impossible. That ship can't move without my conscious will to make it move, and it is prepared against the alien will. It's a scout ship, remember. It's got to have those features or you don't dare send it and me out into the unknown."

"Then you have only to not activate it, and he can do nothing," George pointed out. "At least we can contain the virus here."

"I'm afraid not," I replied carefully. "I'm due back in two years. They'll allow one more, then send *two* scouts out to track me. If neither of those return, then some big guns will go out. And big guns are a hell of a lot sloppier and more ignorant in the face of the unknown than scouts. They'll come down, look around, find things crazy, and do what I did—take some samples and head for home and a panel of experts. They'll take the virus with them, and Moses, still very much alive, will find some way to follow them, directing the virus, seeing through the specimen Choz. No, George, we can't let that happen.

"The only thing we can do is destroy the *Peace Victory* and Moses."

It had turned dark, but we hadn't moved from our shelter up in the valley. It still got chilly here; the virus didn't like the cold, and we were very uncomfortable. Yet we stayed, and we didn't sleep.

"You could ram it," George suggested.

For the ninetieth time I shook my head. "No, that thing's huge. The computer is at the core, armored and protected. Even if we severed the ship in two, there are almost certainly fail-safe systems that would allow it to rejoin, maybe even self-repair. I don't know those ships, but that's the way *I'd* build them, and although the people of your time didn't have the knowledge we do now, they were just as smart."

"I still don't understand why the damn thing needs you at all," George said. "After all, it almost certainly still has strains of the virus in storage."

"The virus, yes," I replied, "but nothing to work from or on. Nor, of course, would it be spreading the Communards—just the virus and some semblance of its original people. No, Moses wants us. And, I think, the only way to handle this is to give him what he wants."

"Huh?" George sounded surprised, and waited for me to continue.

"We've got to go on up there and face him, George," I told him. "We have to convince him he's wrong, bad for humanity, usurping God's role. Yes, that might be the best thing—charge him with blasphemy. We have to talk him out of his power drive before he does something desperate anyway, or before my rescuers arrive."

"What if we can't?" George asked grimly. "What then?"

"Then we'll have to destroy him, somehow. You know the ship and Moses; I don't. That's why I need you. Besides, you're the only one I can trust. Are you game?"

"Curse him to eternal damnation! Yes! Of course!" came the emotional reply.

"Don't curse him," I said softly. "Remember—he's only a machine, just an imperfect mirror of ourselves. We made him what he is—the disease, the cancer."

There was nothing else to say, because that left only cursing ourselves, and we were already cursed.

We stood out there, the two of us, looking at the hill of silvery strands covering the ship.

"Won't he stop us?" George asked nervously.

"No," I told him. "Relax. Remember, we're doing exactly what he wants us to do."

This was the first time I'd ever broken into anything by pissing on it, but that was the way of this world. The acids in the Choz waste dissolved the webbing, which was not very thick. I was afraid for a moment that the two of us wouldn't produce enough to melt the webbing, but we did. There was just enough of a hole to wriggle through, down flat on the ground and inching forward on forelegs alone, rear legs dragging behind.

Since there was no color for metal objects, the ship stood out in sharp, yellow-on-black outline. We found just enough room inside the cocoon to crawl around to the air lock, which was still open exactly as I'd left it so long ago.

"I'll have to go in first," I told George, "and establish a link with the ship. Besides, there's only room for one of us, standing on his tail, in the air lock at one time. The lock may look a little strange, but it works the same as air locks have since time immemorial. Just make sure you clear the grooves on the outside or the outer door will chop your tail off."

I reached the lock, stood up in it, and felt the link with the computer in the ship. Attuned to my brain waves and identity pattern, it would respond only to me and as a part of me as well.

The lock shut, and I almost became a victim of ignoring my own advice. I'm sure several tail hairs were neatly sliced.

When the inner lock finally opened, I entered my home and womb of so long for the first time as an alien. The stark yellow and black of the nonorganic interior plunged me into a world of mist and shadow; only sonar and memory would be my guides.

I *felt* the computer link, *felt* the air lock reopen, and *felt* George enter. Then I closed the outer lock, pressurized, opened the inner, and turned to see a somewhat comforting blue figure enter the cabin.

The place smelled funny and felt uncomfortable, which was strange, too. I hadn't realized until now how really acute my sense of smell was, my ability to detect thousands of scents and to differentiate individuals by them. The place smelled unpleasant, dry, metallic, antiseptic.

Then, too, the temperature and humidity were set for human-norm, too dry and cool for Choz comfort.

"Hang on!" I warned George. "We're busting out of here!"

There was a sensation of lifting and a strong bump as we smashed through the webbing and continued to rise. The pressure was rather uncomfortable. Then, suddenly, we broke free, and the internal systems adjusted to one-G, slightly heavier than we'd been used to and built for but not all that disconcerting.

I immediately caused the thermostat to lower to just a shade above freezing. The temperature dropped so suddenly, in a single blower action, that it came as a terrible shock to us. It must have been an even greater shock to Moses' viruses, suddenly in an environment where they didn't function well at all. We felt no pain, only a terrible urge to do something. The whole world glowed with the danger color, almost a pleading.

And then release.

For the first time, I felt George and I were in complete control.

"God! It's cold!" George muttered, and we could feel it even through our thick, hairy hides.

"Notice something, George?" I called to him, although we were very close. "Turn slightly! Look at me!"

"No color!" he gasped. "You have no color at all! We're strictly on sonar!"

I nodded. "The color was a controlling and programming mechanism. With the virus at least dormant, we're free from old Moses!"

Instinctively I glanced at my screens and instruments, yet, although I was sure they showed what I expected to see, they were blanks to me. The gauges were all covered by plastic, the screens were two-dimensional optical projections.

I edged past George to the bank of dials and gauges I knew blindfolded. I wished that I could see them, see their display readouts, and be reassured, but I could not be. I was flying blind.

Well, so be it, I thought. This ship could fly, if necessary, without me at all, so it would have no problems doing what I ordered—providing nothing broke down.

"How long until we reach the *Peace Victory?*" George asked, shivering from the cold.

"Never, I hope," I told him. "We're not going there. I had no way of telling you and being sure old Moses wasn't listening in, maybe picking things up through the virus strains in my body. We're heading for an outpost communication relay at the edge of claimed territory, about two days away. From there, through the ship, I can contact Seiglein or the government and give them the story. Then we'll blast the hell out of old Moses!"

Ten

"I'm getting something on audio," I called to George. "I bet I know who it is."

George was down in the lower bay, usually my sleeping quarters, trying to orient himself to the interior of the ship I knew so well.

"Moses?" he asked nervously.

"Nobody else it could be," I replied. "Shall we hear what he has to say?"

George was uncertain. "Are you sure you want to? I mean, it's cold as the devil here but who knows what's cold enough? He could be trying to re-establish contact, to force us back."

"Probably," I agreed. "But if he could do it with the virus he'd have done it by now. He's pretty weak at this point; we'll have to make an L-jump soon and that'll put us completely out of range. So let's see what the old boy wants."

Opening audio required me to work a couple of controls. This was difficult without hands, but the hooves separated just far enough to get around the scanning knob. Switches I could throw, although with difficulty, since the forelegs were designed to be feet and provided only a limited freedom of movement.

It took some time and trouble for me to tune him in. Finally, with some whistling and popping, I got him locked in. He had a strange voice, one of the strangest I'd ever heard. It was electronic, yes, but it had a three-dimensional character to it, as if we were listening to a recording of someone that had then been processed to sound electronic. It was an old man's voice—emotional, powerful.

"Please! Please! My children! Respond to my call!" it implored.

I opened the contact switch. "Go ahead, Moses. This is Bar Holliday."

"Why do you do this, my child?" the voice wailed, anguish in its every tone. "Why do you separate yourself from the oneness, run from the great fulfillment of God's holy plan?"

"It's not God's plan," I snapped. "It's yours, Moses. *You* did it. You, alone. You usurped God's powers, his position. You are replacing God, Moses, committing blasphemy."

Not bad for a sure-enough socialist atheist, I thought smugly.

"No! No!" Moses protested. "I am only the agent, only fulfilling God's plan. What I do is God's will. If it were not His will, He would not permit me to do it; he would tell me what to do."

"Bullshit," I replied. "That's the excuse for half the deaths in human history, the wars, the oppression. More people have been killed in the name of God than for any other reason." I liked that—it was one of the few lines I remembered from my history classes.

"But I kill no one!" Moses responded. "No one dies in the colony. I bring only peace, joy without strife."

I sensed George coming up behind me and could almost feel his fury.

"Moses, this is George Haspinol. I was with you from the beginning. You are wrong, Moses. You have sinned."

"Elder Haspinol!" Moses exclaimed. "I do not err. The goals of your holy teachings and those of the holy books are most plain."

"Those goals were not for this life, Moses, but for

the next," George replied sadly. "You have misunderstood."

"I cannot misunderstand," the ship's computer responded obstinately. "I am self-programming, and I think logically as you cannot. All the centuries of the Faith have awaited someone who could properly interpret them. I am that one, the final prophet—the arm of God."

"You've killed them, Moses," I put in. "As sure as if you'd blown them up you've killed them. You killed their humanity, their past. You have made them ignorant animals."

"Animals? No! Far greater than that!" the computer huffed. "True, to enter Eden one must be purified of sin by bathing in the holy waters that take memory. It is the only way, as the Beloved Poet said. But now—now they will be happy, taught to glorify God forever."

I flipped the switch so that we weren't broadcasting.

"It's no use," I told George. "He's a fanatic. He *knows* he has the right answers. He—hey! Hold it!"

"What's the matter?" George asked, alarmed.

"Bless these sensitive long ears!" I yelled. "His signal's getting progressively stronger, but I can't read the instruments! He's been zeroing in on our signal! I have no way of knowing how close he is, so get below and brace yourself as best you can. I'm going to L-jump just as soon as I can!"

Suddenly the fear was back, strong, and I cursed myself for a fool. I had told Moses where we were from our signal, and I'd stopped, waiting for him. Moses could open the loading bays and scoop us in, and I wouldn't have the running-start power I needed to L-jump.

"Braced?" I called nervously to George.

"As good as I can be, considering," was the reply from below.

I ordered straight-line acceleration to put some distance between us and Moses.

Satisfied, I went down on all fours, bracing myself as much as possible against the big padded chair into which I could no longer strap myself, then ordered the L-jump.

It's hard to describe the L-jump to anyone not well versed in physics. The best way, I suppose, is to remember that there are many more dimensions than the four in which we live, each with different properties. Depending on the intersection of those dimensions by the outer hull of the ship, we would be placed under a different set of rules, a different set of physical laws, while an energy cocoon would maintain our own conditions inside. When Igor Kutzmanitov discovered them by accident while studying the strange properties just outside the event horizon of black holes—but, no I'm too technical already. Let's just say that I mentally throw a series of relays and we are suddenly exempt from relativity while speed is multiplied exponentially. It makes for quick trips, weeks or months to places you couldn't reach in hundreds of years at sub-light-speeds.

This would be a short jump, and I actually had to decelerate to match what the ship's computer told me would be the right velocity in L-space to get me where I needed to go. We weren't that far outside explored space. But it would take Moses eighty years to get where we would get in eighty days.

Satisfied, I was almost too complacent as the ship's computer warned of a great mass closing on us fast. Capture would be just a matter of seconds considering my deceleration.

I forced the L-jump.

All signs of matter in the vicinity, vanished. The ship's sensors showed nothing at all now. I'd made it, perhaps with thirty seconds to spare.

The jump itself is a jarring experience, a tremendous bump and bang. I heard George cry out; but the force, so routine when I'm strapped in my chair or bunk was enough to throw me off balance, and I crashed into an auxiliary instrument bank. It was armored, of course, and would survive. But *my* armor was for lighter things, and I felt the sting of several sharp edges cutting into me, not deeply but painfully. I knew that it wouldn't be long before I felt the bruises.

Such sensations were strange to me now. There had been little pain on Patmos, and the virus saw to efficient repair of any damage in a night. But the virus was inactive in the cold, maybe even dead now.

Carefully, I picked myself up. My bushy tail had broken some of the fall, but my right rear foot had been badly twisted. I hoped it wasn't broken.

"George!" I called. "Are you all right?"

"I'm going to ache for a week," he yelled back at me, "but I think I'll survive. You?"

"Cuts and bruises, and my back foot's sprained. Damn! I'd almost forgotten what it was like to feel such pain, and when the shock wears off it'll be worse."

George made his way into the upper-control-room cabin.

"I wish I could look at it, but I'll do what I can," he said. "I was something of a medic, you know, although I'm twenty years out of practice. Lord! Just did a narrow-scan. You've got a couple of nasty cuts there. Some blood, but not much. Where do you keep your medical stores?"

"There's a medicine chest on the wall just before the door to the head," I told him. "But—I don't know if the stuff will work on me now."

"Worth a try," was the reply. I heard him fumbling a lot with something, and deduced that it must be the pull-and-twist handle on the cabinet door. It took him several minutes to manage it without hands, and I'll never know to this day how he did it.

"Lots of stuff in here!" he called finally. The aches

were really coming on strong now, and the hind leg was giving me fits. "Which is the salve?"

"The big jar," I called back. "It's in a recessed holder on the bottom shelf."

"I see it!" he responded. "No way to pick it up, though. Let me see. Hmm . . ." There was silence for a minute more. I felt some wetness on my right side, and knew that I was still bleeding.

Then I heard him coming back up the ramp and into the cabin where I lay. I scanned him and saw that he had the jar in his mouth.

"How did you manage that?" I asked, curiosity overcoming pain.

He put the jar down on the floor and spit some stuff out of his mouth.

"I shot some webbing on it, then ate the line in until I had it," he said matter-of-factly. "But it's too big a jar to get my hoof around. How the hell do we get the top off?"

I stared at the outline of the fat jar on the floor and shook my head slowly. We tried with me holding it between the knees of my forelegs while he pushed, then all sorts of things. Nothing budged it.

I looked up at George, and knew we were both thinking the same thing. For the first time, the very first time, we were both admitting the truth to ourselves. We weren't human anymore. This was a human ship, designed for humans. We were entirely different creatures.

"This isn't going to work, George," I said softly. "We aren't equipped for it."

He nodded glumly. "Here. Lie flat on the floor, hind legs out, tail up on your back," he said grimly. "Let me feel that wound."

I did so, and he ran his forelegs down until he touched the leg.

It hurt like hell, and I almost screamed.

"Broken," he affirmed. "And you're still bleeding. Even the clotting factor is virus-controlled." He paused for a minute. "How long until we get to that beacon?" he asked.

"Eighty days," I replied. "I'll make it, somehow— at least that far."

He was silent again for a while, thinking hard. Finally he said, "No you won't. You'll bleed to death first. And the ship will take me back to base, where I'll be a good zoo animal for somebody. I can't operate your gadgets, you know. Besides, what am I to eat? We'll starve first anyway."

I thought hard through the pain, trying to see a hole in his logic, but I couldn't.

He was right.

"So what do we do?" I asked him. "Go back to Moses? You know we can't. And I can't break an L-jump once committed."

"I think we turn up the heat," he said calmly.

"We don't know what that will do," I objected. "I may have killed the virus. On the other hand, it may be programmed to make us do things."

He stood there a few seconds more, then said the words I most hated in all the universe, even more now because they were so very, very true.

"We have no choice," he said.

I ordered the heat turned up slowly, to give us at least a chance to return to the freeze condition— quickly if necessary.

I felt the heat flow, and it was wonderful. The temperature climbed slowly in the cabin and, as it did, I was tense, looking for nasty influences or signs of change.

There were some of the latter. The color-sense returned intermittently at first, then it came on full. But that didn't help much—just made George a blue tinged with the hue of concern mixed with that of tenseness, probably like my own color. It showed clearly that the virus was still very much alive.

"Feel any strange urges?" I asked him cautiously, still in too much pain to tell anything myself.

"I'm feeling hungry," he replied. "And a hell of a lot more comfortable. That's all."

I chuckled. George was already picking up my bad habits. The preacher was doing some mild cussing.

"I'm going to increase the humidity," I told him. "Temperature's Patmos norm now, near as I can tell."

I brought the humidity up to a level that would be stifling to a human but seemed normal to us.

"Blood flow's slowing," George noted.

I could feel—feel the pain subsiding, had tingling in areas which only moments before had been seas of pain.

"Feeling a little sleepy," I told him. "The repair gang's in all right."

"Go ahead," he urged. "I'll stand watch over both of us."

I slept.

Unable to look at my chronometer, I had no idea how long I'd been out, but the sleep must have been very deep. When I awoke, I felt excellent, refreshed. There was no pain, although I could feel caked blood on my fur.

I looked around. George had finally succumbed, and was snoring soundly nearby. I let him sleep.

I didn't feel any different, I thought, checking myself. Just well again. And hungry.

Or was I different.

The question didn't disturb me as much as it should have, I suppose. I'd already faced it the—night?—before.

The body felt comfortable, normal. I tried to remember being in my human form, yet although the memory was all there, it didn't seem me, really. It was like looking back at someone else, some strange creature I'd once known and befriended, perhaps even liked.

I looked over at George, sleeping peacefully, scanning him slowly.

He looked normal to me. *He* was people.

An effect of the virus? I wondered. No, probably not. I recalled people living on a hellhole of a world only theoretically Terraformed. The smell in the atmosphere, while not harmful, was revolting. I had to wear an air mask. But the people—born there, born with that smell as a part of their normal existence—hadn't even noticed it. Even the old-timers, born off-world, had adapted.

I'd seen cold worlds where temperatures I could hardly bear were normal, where people lived and loved and worked without a thought. Man had colonized a hundred such worlds, most of them very different from the world he'd come from. Even Earth—I recalled the extremes of climate and altitude that they'd said was there. People who always lived near the poles on the ice cap. People who lived at elevations so high that other men couldn't even breathe comfortably.

We adapt. That's why man has survived and spread and dominated.

We adapt even to another form, I thought. Take to it as if it were our own.

If *I* felt this way, what of George? How long had I been nonhuman? Three months? Four? For him, it was twenty years, twenty years removed from humanity.

I took a look at the strangely and cruelly formed alien creature sleeping over there, and I knew that I was an alien, too.

The virus was an analog of a mechanical computer, of course. It had been programmed and it would follow in that program. Even here, cut off completely from Moses' influence, it continued to do its job. And with that realization came the added knowledge that, if Moses were destroyed as he must be, I would spend the rest of my very long life as this creature.

Or would it be a long life? I wondered suddenly.

What were we to eat for this trip—and back? No
grass and tubers here. I considered our predicament
for a moment. How would we have eaten on Moses'
ship? Would I have ferried soil and seeds up there?
The place had been cleared out, and he needed organic material to work with.

Suddenly, curiously, I had to go to the bathroom.
It was the last thing I needed—to get emptier—but
I sighed and rose, trying not to make a clatter with
my hooves as I went downstairs to the head.

When I got there, I discovered another problem. The
head was small; obviously. It needed only to be a
little place to sit. For a man to sit.

I just didn't fit into it. For one thing, even getting
myself in ass-end first, I couldn't get over the seat. My
rear aimed down between my legs.

The pressure was becoming unbearable, as it does
when you gotta go and have to hold it, and I looked
around anxiously for some place to put it. I was still
considering my problem when nature forced the is-
sue, and out it came onto the floor, loads of it.

When finished, I turned and looked around, as
animals sometimes do. Using the implanted instincts
of the virus, I did what all Choz do, and spread it
out thinly until it covered quite a space. Stopping
to think, I considered that this was going to be a messy
trip—or would be, if we had any food to make more
waste.

Maybe we did, I thought suddenly. The probe still
held the original soil sample, that part of it not used
in analysis. There would also be the inevitable grass
containing its tiny seeds. Virus-controlled, it grew almost overnight, replenishing what the Choz of the
field consumed the previous day.

Again the effort took some work. I had to operate
controls not designed for me in order to lift the probe
core to the plastic, vacuum-insulated viewing case.
I knew it was there, heard it click in despite not being able to sound it. Now I just had to get it into this

atmosphere, into the ship proper. This was a problem, since the case was designed to keep it out.

I hammered at it with my foreleg, but it only went *thump, thump, thump* against the hard plasticine bubble. First of all, I could only lift my forelegs, and they bent only inward. No pressure could be exerted by them except when weight was on them.

The run! I thought suddenly. Those big, powerful rear legs with a kick that could propel me many meters across the plains in one leap!

I turned, aimed as best I could, and, bracing myself on my forelegs, kicked hard. Again! Again! And again!

The noise woke George, who called out to me in concern.

"No problems!" I assured him, hoping that was true. I told him what I was trying to do.

Back at it again. Kicking blind, I bent in a good deal of the side as well, but I didn't care if a few cabinets I could no longer use got smashed.

Suddenly I had it, heard it crack and shatter.

I turned, and the probe stood exposed among shattered bubble fragments. It was partially open, so no problem there.

George came down, and the two of us struggled to get the big ball, now open slightly on invisible hinges, out and onto the floor. Dirt and some grass fell out. The pinkness was almost too much, but, with willpower, we managed to get the stuff to my fertilizer patch.

The release of tension being what it was, George had the same problem as I had had and added his fecal matter to the field.

We spent an agonizing day and night, consumed with hunger, checking on the patch constantly. Nothing else was on either of our minds. We could see that the virus was still there, and that it knew its job. Some of it, too, would have been in our fecal matter, and it would, we hoped, know our need.

The process began, accelerated, and became fascinating to watch.

The material grew all right, forming a patch of pink on the floor, but not nearly enough for the two of us. As we watched, it increased its growth even more, developing at speeds far beyond anything normal, dying, falling, and providing nurse material for new growth.

The virus was doing to the little sample what it had done to change me—speeding up cellular division to an enormous rate, using the new organic matter to create more.

"Where does it get the energy to do that?" I wondered.

"From the lights," George replied. "Just like our plants get it from the sun. It takes that radiated energy and converts it to matter. We're going to eat again, Bar!"

I was watching my former bedroom and lounge become a jungle.

"Yeah," I replied, still glum. "So now how do we stop it?"

Eleven

Stopping the process proved easy. I could still control the lights and their intensity. When we'd spread the humus around and gotten a pretty good patch growing, enough to feed us and some left over, I turned down the lights. The growing slowed. Without that energy, the virus could do only so much.

Some experimentation established the proper light level. We had to get water to the plants, of course, but that proved fairly easy. We just cooperated in working the washbasin, George holding the tap down. I would then lap up the water but not swallow it, and spit it over as much of the field as I could. I kept the humidity at almost maximum so the soil remained reasonably moist.

And, as the days went by, we helped by fertilizing our own field.

To human, civilized minds this all might sound grotesque, disgusting. But we were starving, for one thing, and, for another, we were not human and we were close to the earth. All of this was a normal and necessary part of existence.

Only four days out I started feeling strange. First, there was the additional motion in the vicinity of my stomach; occasionally I would feel bruised down there. Then, too, I seemed weaker than normal, much more so than could be explained by past injuries.

I mentioned it to George and he laughed.

"Sure! You've just been working and worrying too much to notice or remember. Look, scan my pouch."

93

I did, and it seemed enlarged and irregular. On impulse I did the same to myself. Yes, what I'd feared was a growth was there, only this was the first time I'd noticed that George's condition matched my own.

"The eggs have hatched!" the older man laughed. "Remember? You got one in the Breed, I'm sure. So did I. We're going to be papas in a couple of days!"

Somehow I'd just forgotten that experience, or overlooked it anyway. Now the evidence became too much to ignore. It wasn't exactly being pregnant, but it was close enough.

I remembered Mara's description of the Breed's aftermath.

"Hey!" I protested. "It was supposed to be out in eight to ten days! It's been longer than that."

"Probably the freezing," George guessed. "Remember, we are not independent organisms—we exist in symbiosis with the virus. Turn off the virus and you turn off most of the processes it controls. Humans have gene patterns to direct this sort of thing; we don't. The virus replaces the genes, the DNA in the cells—or, at least, their function."

I nodded. It didn't bother me as much now that the invisible partner was no longer controlled by an outside intelligence. Left alone, the reconstructed mutated virus was doing what its own DNA and RNA molecules directed and no more—which did give rise to a disturbing thought, though.

"George, what if somebody else knew about our viruses? Couldn't they take us over?"

He shook his head. "I doubt it. Remember, there's more to this than just knowing about the things. You have to know what to tell them to do, and, most important how. And, of course, they were designed to Moses' specifications. I suppose it's possible, though, with a lot of time and a lot of guinea pigs."

This concept gave me pause. "George, there's a whole planetload of guinea pigs back there once

Moses is destroyed. We might have added a new wrinkle to Seiglein Corporation's repertoire."

He considered this for a while. Finally he looked up at me and said, seriously, "Bar? Do we dare do what we're doing?"

This question bothered me as well, but I knew the answer.

"You know we do," I told him. "This is the lesser of two evils. After all, we *know* what will happen eventually if we don't. We don't know how *they'll* react. We can only hope they'll blow Moses and let us run the planet."

Four days later the children emerged. Not all at once, just the head first. With no horns—thank goodness!—they had the preprogrammed color-sense and hearing but little else. Even so, when I ate, junior leaned out and ate as well. George's emerged not a day after mine, looking identical according to my senses.

George was the expert here, and I followed his example. Even while the young were in the pouches, their education began. It consisted mostly of George, then me, saying words like "food" and "eat" when the kid was in the proper position or doing the thing we labeled.

We labeled everything. After a few days it got to be a habit, and it seemed to work very well.

Mine grew fast, and weighed exceedingly heavy on me. In short order he could no longer retract completely into the pouch, was always head out, then head and forelegs. This forced me to go on all fours all the time; it was too awkward to balance. My only solace was that George, who'd done this many times before, was having the same problems.

Although mine had been the first to emerge, George's was the first to drop, and he sighed with obvious relief. The kid still had only small nubs of horns and no real vision, and so had to be guided around; but the little guy was developing with the rapidity that only the Choz could experience. Twelve or more years of growth and development was being done at six times normal speed. You couldn't actually see them grow and develop, but every day the kids changed.

Mine dropped the day after George's, and we discovered why it'd taken so long. It was a female, and females were smaller.

"No doubt about it," George said after turning the kid over and looking to make sure. "You're a real freak, Bar. But it figures. Remember, Moses expected you to return to the ship: you're the only one who could; the only one who he could be sure of; and you're the only one he had particular control over when changing."

We understood, now, how Moses planned to build up his population while carrying his seed to distant stars.

"It's a wonder he didn't make *me* female, like he did some of your original crew," I remarked.

"No, he thought it through," George replied. "You only need one male, you know, and you were the only one he was certain would come to the ship, the only one *able* to come."

We named George's boy Ham, in the older man's one-syllable tradition and, I found out, from his holy book. My daughter he talked me into calling Eve, since she was woman out of man, some story from his book again.

It was okay with me. I wasn't used to being a father.

The children were a welcome addition nonetheless, since it helped jam the seemingly endless days in L-jump. No two Choz, even the Seconds, had ever gotten so much attention, or so much teaching. Both were already miniature versions of full Choz, and speaking sentences after a fashion by the time the eightieth day rolled around. Ham and Eve had been so much of an experience, and so welcome a diversion, that we'd thought little of the ethical problems and possible consequences up to now.

A warning buzzer sounded through the ship, signaling emergence from the jump in ten minutes. It was so strange an intrusion, and we were so divorced from any real sense of time, that it took me a moment to realize what it was.

The kids ran to us, fearing the new, unknown sound, unusually harsh and irritating to our fine-tuned, full-range hearing.

"It'll be another big bump," I warned George, and turned to the kids. "A big bang is coming," I told them softly. "It won't hurt, but it can toss you around and hurt you that way."

This time we had a field down below with soft grasses, and we lay down in it, bracing ourselves and the kids against one another.

The buzzer sounded again at regular intervals. I counted them off.

"Ten . . . nine . . . eight . . . seven . . . six . . . five . . . four . . . three . . . two . . . one . . ." *Bang!* The whole ship shook and shuddered, and we bounced around a good deal, but even though we all slid toward a wall we were ready for it this time and able to break the fall. The kids were scared and crying, and we comforted them first.

That done, I checked the computer. We were still some distance from the beacon—I'd had to guess fast on the jump—and we proceeded toward it in normspace. I could already hear it—or, rather, the computer could hear it and send that information to me— a constant, wailing tone, very distant.

It took us two days to reach it.

I knew the beacon well, since I'd placed it there last time out. And the one to which it sent as well— and the one before that. This was my territory, had been for ten years.

The beacons were unmanned outposts in the dark,

giving a homing signal, even living quarters for a long period if rescue was what was needed. And, they could shoot a message cylinder, passing it on down the line in L-jump to the next station, at velocities much faster than any human could stand.

Such a message would reach a Seiglein station in a matter of hours. The time lag then would depend on how quickly the message was decoded, interpreted, and an answer formulated by higher-ups. An immediate reply would be plus or minus seven hours, so it would be a long conversation and I was sure there'd be many questions.

Now, suddenly, the old nerves were coming back.

"What do I tell them, George?" I asked, concerned. "And how much?"

He chewed on his lip a moment.

"I've been thinking about that the last few hours," he responded slowly. "We have to tell them the truth. Will there be a visual?"

I nodded. "It's automatic."

"Okay, then, you tell them everything. Spare no details. Make it as dramatic as you can—you're living proof of the truth. But leave out me and the kids— we'll stay back here in the ship."

I looked at him strangely. "Bad feeling?"

He shrugged. "Call it caution. Alone, you're no threat. Four of us—one a female—that's a threat. Think about Eve."

I saw his point and agreed.

The computer automatically connected to the beacon air lock, and I could hear the thrumming of motors as the atmosphere was released from storage and the pressure was equalized. Finally, the air lock opened, then the outer one, and I hopped, hooves clattering against the bare ribbed metal floor, into the beacon station. There was no color, there being no organic material other than me in the place. I scanned and quickly discovered what I was looking for.

The broadcast console was hard to manage. For

one thing, there was a fixed, padded chair in front of it with positioned microphone and cameras. I wasn't built to fit there, and I had to squeeze in as best I could. Furthermore, the controls lacked the identifying markers that would have shown me which was which. I didn't get into these things much and they changed them every once in a while. The labels were there, all right. They were just flat printing, and I couldn't read them.

The problem with the chair, the mikes, and the controls caused me to have problems just reaching the panel, and my hooves certainly didn't make for easy adjustment, even when guessing which control was which. I knew there was even a picture diagram for those unfamiliar with the equipment, but, again, I couldn't see or read it.

Finally I got everything turned on, hoped my position and the controls were all right, and reported in, telling the story briefly and as best I could. Then it took some more time to find the transmit switch, and two tries to hit it. I was wondering if I blew it, when I felt a shudder go through the station as the projectile was ejected.

The kids wanted to explore the new place, but I was leery as to how much was being broadcast and recorded, and kept them out.

We ate, played with the kids a little until it was time to go back to the beacon station. The little shudder and bump told me that a return message had arrived.

Fourteen hours, I thought. It had no meaning. Time had no meaning anymore.

Well, I'd guessed right on transmit, so I tried the complementary control that just had to be *Receive*—and it was.

"Beacon 1458936-YL," came a human voice—the first human voice I'd ever heard as a Choz. It sounded harsh, throaty, unpleasant. "We have received a blank message cylinder from you. Please listen and follow our instructions, watching the screen to do as we do, so we can receive you properly. If we do not receive a message from you within fifteen standard hours we will dispatch a ship, never fear."

I cursed under my breath. What could I have done wrong? I wanted this over and done with.

The pictorial example was useless, of course, but the voice instructions were quite complete. I went through the whole procedure with them and found that I had done it all right. Oh, maybe the level was off, but, if so, it was on the high side.

Then, of course, I understood. First, not being able to see anything except by sonar, I'd neglected to turn on the camera lights! Second—well, why no voice transmission? I shook my head and went back to George.

"I don't know," was all the help he could offer. "Unless—maybe our speech is different somehow."

"Of course it is!" I sighed, and cursed myself for a fool.

Our speech was entirely ultrasonic, of course. The whole story was on the cylinder, all right, but the men at the other end didn't have the playback equipment to get at it. The recording range was designed for human speech and compressed to fit the storage requirements.

I thought about the problem and thought about it some more. For numerous reasons I didn't want to meet that rescue ship, which, in any event, would be a good half a year away unless they had somebody closer. Three months anyway.

"I can't understand how Moses could hear us," George noted. "After all, didn't the same limitations also apply to him?"

"No," I responded. "He was picking us up directly, receiving us by his own transceiver from our numberless internal, biological transceivers. We eventually got *him* with a radio and just assumed he was getting us the same way."

The Web of the Chozen

Then I had the solution. The ship's computer was almost literally a part of me. *It* had its own voice, of course, for broadcast at a beacon station when the pilot was dead.

I scanned the computer logic and told it what I wanted. It complied with a direct link into the station.

The only trouble was, I couldn't be on visual in the station and talking through the computer in the ship.

So, of course, we sent George in to smile for the cameras. They wouldn't know the difference.

Once again I told the story, again I made the omissions about my own family here and about my own feelings of literal alienation from them. I needed Moses destroyed, and only they could do it.

After, we ate a little, then slept. Schedules were for the humans, and the beacon.

The second return message was quite different, and an hour late.

"Holliday!" said a voice that sounded terrible, evil, monstrous to me. "This is—to put it mildly—hard to believe. That—that creature is now you?" It broke off a moment, then continued. "Well—we will certainly send a force out! That an old computer—well, it's hard to accept, but there you are and there this story is."

There was another pause. I was troubled by a certain slight familiarity in the voice even though it sounded so strange.

The voice—a woman's, I realized—continued. "Well, now, we'll proceed to the beacon immediately and from there to this Patmos to solve this, er, situation. Wait for us."

For Seiglein to take possession of their new pets?

Not me.

Suddenly I recognized the voice. It had once sounded sweet to me, even pretty, although that was hard to imagine now.

It was Olag 4516 Brosnyak.

I tried to visualize her, remember her as she was

101

when I walked out on her two years before. That was somehow hard to do. Was even memory a victim of this process? I wondered.

Oh, I remembered what she looked like, the whole relationship, which we knew was only a between-mission thing. She belonged too much to the Corporation, and I belonged to no one but myself.

I dismissed the memory as unimportant. The reply was important, and we worked it the same way.

"Good to see you, Olag," I began, trying to sound as human as possible. "Yes, the first intelligent alien mankind has made contact with is me. Look, I want to see all this go down, and I want to be there after to talk about what will happen. Pardon me if I remind you of our talks about my faith in anything, most of all the Corporation. You have the coordinates. I'll wait another fifteen for your reply, then, no matter what it says, I'm off for Patmos. Don't be so shocked, either, at the way I look. Look at the people's faces in those apartments near your office, staring into their Creativisions, munching their nutritious food cubes. At least some of *these* people still talk to each other, and watching grass grow is at least as constructive. See you."

I signed off, and George pushed the transmit button. I felt the shudder, and knew the capsule was off.

We went through another entire eat-teach-eat-sleep cycle before there was a reply. This time it wasn't Olag —it was somebody higher up. Another woman, but she sounded even more monstrous and evil.

Must be a Seiglein, I thought acidly.

"All right, Holliday," the stranger said, and I wished I could see what she looked like. "You win. Your psych profile and record indicate that you are as crazy and as antisocial as scouts usually are—that's why you're out there, and we're here, and you're in this mess looking like that."

Pig's ass, I thought. If any of those toadies from the Corporation had been on Patmos they'd be singing halleleujahs with Moses and loving it now. But, of course, that was the other reason why I was out here and they were back there.

"Now, we recommend that you do not get too close to the *Peace Victory* before we handle the matter. After all, if what you say is true the computer can regain control of you. You will be our check that the computer is dead. The *PV* was made by Macklock back on Earth and we don't have all the plans and information on it we'd like. It was a long time ago."

I smiled. I didn't get out here to go back the fool, I thought. I would be there, and we'd all be in the freezer.

I'd neglected to tell them a few other things, too.

"You are getting the Cruiser *Courrant* under Gerald Alois Seiglein himself, along with two destroyers. After the *PV* is destroyed, approach and stand off the *Courrant* and we will attend to you."

That was it, the end of the message.

And I didn't like the end line at all.

Like hell I was going to come under those guns! Particularly not for second grandson Gerald Alois Seiglein.

Twelve

We laid off about two-thirds of the way to Patmos. Actually, I was in something of a bind, since I had no clear time sense and didn't dare stick near the beacon nor go back to the vicinity of Moses. Fortunately, the timing mechanism for the L-jump was adaptable as a stopwatch of sorts, and my own calculations said that if Seiglein were coming he would be coming from Altara, his family's private little fiefdom, and that would take one hundred ninety-seven days.

There was no hurry. We used the time well in teaching Ham and Eve, and we were very careful in the way in which it was done. This was, after all, the first time two Choz Seconds or later could be taught off-planet, in isolation, and it was a golden opportunity to tell them the right things.

One thing, for sure, was to avoid the initial mistakes of the Communards. Shocked by their new status, they had taught the Seconds as humans and had, in the process, painted something of an idealized view of the older race, the race with hands, with choice in sex, with optical vision—whatever that was. Not having experienced it, the young naturally had fantasized it into something marvelous.

Of course, these attitudes had been passed down as much as the rapid breeding would allow, losing any correspondence to reality in the translation, becoming ever more inflated.

Those who'd seen me land, the Seconds, Thirds, and so on, had felt sorry for me, pitied me for being transformed into one of them, a god suddenly stripped of power and position and cast among the damned.

That explained why I got a lot of respect and little resistance.

These children wouldn't be like that.

We were determined that they would accept themselves for what they were, a different species; that they would regard man as an alien race, different, certainly, for that is what alien means, but not better nor worse than they. We were careful to tell them of the colony of Patmos as a history of a new race, not the remains of a discarded old one. They were not human, they would never be human. The humans were those folks Over There someplace, the funny ones who depended entirely on machines and didn't have some of the wondrous things that the Choz had.

The process worked well, really, although it was unsettling to see them so receptive from the start and grow so quickly toward adulthood. Unlike human babies, they were almost reasoning recorders (the better to memorize scripture, eh Moses?) who absorbed all that we threw at them. And, in our tiny, closed environment, they took all we said at face value, having nothing to compare it with.

The only thing we couldn't really convey was the deep appreciation of and feeling for nature; they had never been off my ship. That would come later, the joy of discovery of the freedom of the Choz on the plain.

George and I often wondered what would have been the colony's fate, shape, and health now if they had started with the Seconds like this and had this sort of close, intimate, moment-to-moment relationship with every Choz child during the formative first two years.

And, finally, as all good things must, the buzzer warned me that it was time. The old, nervous gut feelings were back. The fear was there, that nameless, shapeless thing that was in every thinking creature at one point or another: fear of the unknown.

The whole future of a race would be decided soon,

we knew, and there was no clear way to predict how these things would go. How would Moses react? How would Seiglein?

In the interim we'd also been able to selectively grow and partially bale some grass as cushions; the L-jump wouldn't be as much of a threat this time out.

"Are we going to Patmos now?" Eve asked me, excited and anxious.

I nodded. "Yes, I hope so, Eve," I responded as cheerfully as I could manage.

They remembered the previous L-jump and needed no coaxing to get into cushioning positions. I triggered it, and we managed to get through it with only minor, quickly healable bruises. Hooves, it must be noted, hurt as much when jabbed into you as metal abutments.

I also had to warn them about lowering the temperature. About 1°C felt safe enough, but it would also slow down our food supply. I hoped we wouldn't have to worry about that for long. I cooled us down just before emergence and made sure that we had a full-grown crop in our lounge garden.

The cold and excitement made us ignore any problems with the bump out of the jump this time.

I set the ship's scanners on full around. We were still some distance from Patmos, too far to spot it, but I would have picked up the human force's signals if they had arrived. They hadn't, and I had to consider how long we could exist in this cold, unprotected condition waiting for them.

I took a nav fix and found that we were probably within Moses' receptor range. I quickly headed us out of there after putting some more distance between us, set the sensors on standby so that I wouldn't be caught off guard by the computer again.

"How long do you think it'll be?" George asked apprehensively.

I shook my head. "I have no idea. If Baby Seiglein is true to form, he waited until he loaded his pet press and Creativision crews. If the boy comes out of the retreat, it's to full bands and fanfares."

Ham looked over at me. "You don't like them very much, do you, Bar?"

"The Seigleins?" I responded with a snigger. "Hardly!"

"No, no," he replied innocently. "The humans."

I'd picked it pretty good at that. Three days later, sensors picked up three objects emerging from the L-jump in mild disarray. This was all to the good—we were miserably cold, had gotten little sleep, and our cautious nibbling at the now dormant grasses and tubers only made us hungrier.

The three ships—two standard navy vessels and a monster that could only have been the *Courrant*—quickly arranged themselves into standard formation and headed toward Patmos.

Nervously I tried to guess the *Courrant*'s range. The little babies I'd cut my teeth on, but the monsters were few and far between and I'd never even been on one.

"I wish we could see what was going on," Eve complained, and I agreed with her. There was little I could do on that score—despite the fact that it sounds like it to laymen, the link with my ship wasn't by some sort of telepathy; rather, it was a symbiosis in many ways as complete as that between the virus and the Choz. Through its sensors I could follow the ships as dots on a screen; the images were fed directly to my brain. But that would be it.

"Well," I murmured. "Maybe you can't see, but you can hear it." I opened up the communications channels on the Seiglein frequency.

". . . to Channel 161, B mode . . ." came a tinny, unpleasant voice. "Repeating this recording: To Bar Holliday. You are to switch to the battle frequency. Turn to Channel 161, B mode . . ." came the full message, which started to repeat a third time.

I switched, one of those operations requiring a manual resetting of four dials, and, with hooves, terribly tough on the middle dials. I managed; when you know the frequency and channel you're starting from it's easier to count the digits than to move the wheels.

I chose a million kilometers to trail them. This was outside the range of just about anything I'd ever heard of short of a robomissile—and I'd have a small time lag in communications. Well, that lag would be enough for an emergency L-jump if I spotted anything hurled at us. I set it up, random pattern, to activate just in case.

Scouts were the expendable property of Seiglein. I didn't *think* he'd do anything rash, but you never knew.

"Holliday here on 161," I called. "Tracking you, task force."

"Affirmative, Scout Holliday," came the reply— Olag, I noted with amusement. Something had finally pried her out of that velvet cocoon.

The star the Patmosians called Christmas was now visible, and, with adjustments for my scope range, I could pick out the planets, particularly the all-important number four, Patmos itself.

"I intercepted him between planets two and three," I warned them. "Stationary orbit. However, he has full motive power and he chased me nicely. Watch it—I don't think anybody's built a computer like that one since."

"For which we can all be thankful," Olag responded, a touch of nervousness in her voice. I smiled inwardly at this; about time some of the desk jockeys found out what being human was really all about.

How I would have loved, this once, to have scanned her face and aura!

We approached cautiously; the wide scan field of the *Courrant* almost reached me, as far back as I was. I saw it as little ripples on the screen.

Either Seiglein had a good captain or he wasn't a bad admiral.

"Nothing so far," reported Olag, tension building in her every word.

I laid off and they made a complete circuit of the orbit. When they reappeared on the other side of Christmas still alone, I knew Moses wasn't there.

"Doesn't make sense," George said to me. "I can't imagine that he'd desert them like that. He has too much of a sense of responsibility for the colony."

I nodded. "Agreed. He's here somewhere, and he knows we're all here. I think he's just feeling us out. Whoops! Wait a minute!"

"Large UHVO closing fast, three o'clock," came a crisp male voice—one of the destroyers, almost certainly.

I checked. It wasn't Moses—too small for that—but it was a large chunk of rock, a small planetoid, and it was *fast,* like it had been shot from a great cannon. It closed rapidly on the fleet, which didn't budge. Their energy shielding was already deployed.

"Locked on," came another, different male voice. "Go!"

A strong beam, like lightning, lashed out from the bow of the *Courrant,* striking the object squarely. It reacted as if it had hit a wall, then split into several small chunks thrown by recoil in all directions but forward.

The charge hadn't been strong enough to completely destroy the rock, but it had done the job. I calculated the trajectory of the pieces, found none would come close enough to worry about, and promptly ignored them.

"They just shot the rock away," I told my three anxious listeners in the downstairs lounge. "That thing was almost two kilometers around and he just pushed it away. There's a lot of power on that big baby."

"I wonder how much?" George mused, mostly to himself. Then he called up to me, "Hey! Bar! Where do you suppose the thing came from?"

"Jillions of them in space," I responded. "Could be just chance."

But I doubted it.

Instantly I was replaying the previous scene, reversing trajectory on the object. From Planet Six—no, near Six, really. Too close not to have been affected by the giant gas ball's gravity if it had been that close on its own.

I knew that the task force had already done the same thing, and saw them move out.

"It's Moses, testing weaponry," I reported to the Choz. "He slingshot the thing around the planet."

"What's a slingshot?" I heard Eve ask, and George explained the term in context without ever telling her what a slingshot really was.

"He's four kilometers long," I murmured under my breath. "Dammitall, he can't hide forever."

But he wasn't there when they got there, and there was no telltale energy trace to show where he'd been.

Where the hell was Moses hiding?

Seiglein must have been thinking along similar lines. I heard Olag say, "Okay, we're sure it was a slingshot at us, a test. Deploy and root him out. He's got to be so close in to the planet that he's beyond our sensor pickup."

They broke, the huge *Courrant* standing off station while the two destroyers did a sweep. I watched as one rounded the big planet, waiting for him to emerge around the other side.

"Nothing yet," came the first male voice. "Still I—"

Suddenly the transmission was cut off.

"*Deputy, Deputy,* do you read? Come in, please! Report!" Olag pleaded.

There was silence.

"*MacAlester,* rendezvous with *Courrant,*" came the sudden, terse order from the mother ship. The remaining destroyer broke off and joined up with the big ship, about a kilometer off the big one's screens.

"Does that mean they *lost* one?" George asked incredulously.

"I think so," I replied almost absently, mind glued to the scan.

"But how is that possible?" George persisted. "Moses isn't armed!"

I sighed. "He's got a mouth," I reminded the old Choz. "He tried to swallow us. I think he gobbled up the destroyer. If he did, they couldn't use any weapons without blowing themselves to bits as well."

"But couldn't they talk?" Eve cut in. "I mean, why can't we hear them?"

"I don't know, honey," I responded honestly. "But, like I said, there's never been a computer like this before or since."

"Bar! We've lost *Deputy!*" Olag called to me.

"I heard," I told her. "I warned you about this son of a bitch." Quickly, I told her and the *MacAlester* what I thought happened.

"Well, then, they'll get a signal to us somehow and we'll have him," she said confidently.

"Uh uh, O-O," I responded drily. "Think about it. What would you do if you spotted the bastard now?"

"Zap him," came the coldly determined answer from the *MacAlester* captain on our party line.

"Right," I responded. "So if it was you in that thing, would *you* broadcast? You suicidal?"

They all considered that.

"So he's got hostages, then," Olag said at last.

"Maybe," I told them. "Maybe not. He's smart enough not to count on anybody holding fire just because some of our own are there. No, he's got something potentially more valuable to him."

"What do you mean?" almost everyone, including those below on my ship, asked.

"He still has the primal samples of that virus, remember," I said softly. "He's got a nice little chemical bank for making a lot of it fast. Right now I'll bet the *Deputy*'s covered with it. They're analyzing the

111

metallic structure, the composition all the way down to the atomic. They're feeding all this information to Moses, and Moses is figuring how to eat his way inside, to the men and women on that ship. How big's the crew?"

"Thirty," she replied.

I nodded. "Thirty trained and knowledgeable people and Moses—hell, he'll have a field day. Don't forget the Communards."

There was silence this time, as they considered the implications and didn't like what they were thinking.

Suddenly there was an override. "Admiral Seiglein here to all crew on all units," came a voice that sounded slightly weird and stupid to me but probably did to them, too. Jerry Seiglein suffered from permanent adolescence in some things.

"Look, the longer we let this thing sit, the better off that computer will be," he noted with a logic that surprised me. Maybe he *did* have something on the ball after all. "Holliday? Could he figure out how to operate the *Deputy* once inside?"

I considered it. "Doubtful," I told him. "Even if he could reason out the controls, there's the mind-key, you know. He can't get into your thoughts, only into your emotions and muscle reactions."

Seiglein didn't hesitate. "Holliday, fear's an emotion. So is claustrophobia, at least it can be physically induced. Besides, military ships can't be on mind-lock—somebody else must always be able to command in an emergency!"

And he was right, I realized suddenly. They were open mechanicals. If Moses could figure out the controls, he could lock into the control computer and use it.

"Admiral, is *Deputy*'s construction on the molecular level similar to my ship?" I asked.

"Identical," came the reply.

"Then you'd better get him now," I warned. "He had almost three months to study this ship. He already knows most of what he needs to know, and he's inside now, Admiral. All he's trying to do is neutralize the crew and figure out the controls."

"Close group!" Seiglein ordered, and I knew this meant that both ships were now under the bridge command of the *Courrant*. I was glad I wasn't on the *MacAlester.*

The destroyer moved out ahead of the bigger ship but not too far, and they both moved slowly across the face of the gas giant in tight formation. I started adjusting my own ship to keep them in view. Then, suddenly, so quickly that I couldn't follow it until it was over, I saw the quarry.

But which *was* the quarry?

The smaller *Deputy,* its blip slightly irregular from norm, shot out and collided with the *MacAlester,* while the huge bulk of the *Peace Victory* plowed through the energy screens of the *Courrant* stern-first, crashing into the larger ship. The bulk was not equal; the *Courrant,* large as it was, was barely a quarter the size of the *PV.*

The radio was bedlam.

The *Courrant* had a gash in her side; not fatal, but they would take a few precious minutes to get everything straightened out.

"Infidels!" roared Moses on Channel 161 via the smashed *Deputy.*

"Children of Satan you are punished now!"

And, with that, I watched as the *Peace Victory* maneuvered more tightly than I would have believed possible for such bulk, the front bay open now, swallowing both the crumpled remains of *Deputy* and the still intact but out of control *MacAlester.* Then, suddenly, there was full boost and he was off my screen.

"Courrant! Courrant!" I called. "Olag! What's your situation?" I had never felt so helpless: tiny, unarmed, and threatened. I opened screens wide, not wanting a huge shape to add me to its collection.

George and the kids clamored to know just what was

going on, but I had more important things to find out.

Finally there was a crackling and I heard Seiglein's voice. It sounded even more strained, cracked—and furious. "Holliday! We'll be fully operational in about one more minute. We've got a lock on the *Peace Victory* but our drives are damaged. He knew just where to hit us!"

"Can you L-jump?" I asked him.

"Affirmative," he replied. "But we've lost too much fuel for a sublight pursuit and he's headed out-system."

So Moses was making tracks with his prize, I thought. Abandoning us, abandoning Patmos.

Ironically, the *Courrant* couldn't go *slow* enough to give chase. They had enough power for in-system work, and probably enough reserve for an L-jump, although they probably wouldn't make the second beacon before they would have to call for help, being unable to match proper velocity for a full jump.

I felt the *Courrant*'s extraordinarily powerful scan beams lock on me, even at this distance. I realized that in the excitement of battle I'd moved inside the seven-hundred-thousand K mark. And the *Courrant* was now moving—moving slowly toward me.

I started moving back, using my greater speed.

"Bar!" a shaken Olag called. "Don't move away! We have to link up now!"

Even receding, I felt the aiming pulse from *Courrant* as the weapons systems locked onto me.

"Please, Bar!" Olag called. "I want to see you again. Talk over old times. We want to help you, Bar. Don't move away."

Four robomissiles fired, and I tracked them at a little over a half-million K and closing fast. I made the emergency L-jump.

The screens blanked.

Thirteen

George and the kids grumped a little about the bouncing I had given them, but they calmed down when I told them the reason. I wasn't feeling too great myself, but I had managed a brace of sorts.

"But why would they want to kill us?" Ham asked, genuinely confused and distressed.

I considered my answer a moment.

"Because we're different, Ham, that's why. People fear anything that is different. They don't know us, and anything they don't know is a threat to them."

"Patmos," George put in, voice cracking. "What will they do to poor Patmos?"

"I don't know," I replied honestly. "We'll have to find out, of course. Remember, the one thing the planet's people don't have is mobility. They're stuck there." That Seiglein would not harm Patmos because of the Choz' lack of space-flight was a ray of hope that I wanted to believe, but couldn't, quite. Maybe if Moses had been destroyed, yes, but—now? And with the Seiglein temper?

I had jumped only an hour, so we were still fairly close when we emerged, although too far to receive real-time radio signals. I could still make out the system, but just barely.

George came up behind me, and I glanced around at him.

"So what do we do now?" the older man asked.

"Wait," I replied. "The only thing we *can* do. Give

Seiglein a while, then go back and check. We can't make any plans until then."

"You don't think they'll wait to blast us?" he responded nervously.

I shook my head. "Doubtful. Baby Seiglein's had a nasty taste of Moses and he can't count a hundred percent on the old boy staying away, although I think he will. He's exposed now, and slow—he'll run, the better the distance, the less likelihood of being found. As for the *Courrant*, the shields helped a little but the ship *is* damaged, and leaking a little fuel. They'll jump for the beacon as soon as they can to save themselves and perhaps come back later if they want."

"Can you tell when they leave?" Eve asked, curious. My routine link with the ship was mysterious to all of them; it gave me some power they could not share.

"I've set the energy detection screen, so when they jump I'll know if it's anywhere within half a light-year. There's a lot of energy used when you jump," I told her.

A few cycles later, the ship signaled for me to come to the bridge. I was surprised; although my time sense was shot, it was certainly a lot sooner than I'd expected them to jump.

They hadn't. The energy bursts were too small for an L-jump, and too regular. These signals were coming from within the system, and I'd never in my life experienced anything quite like them. This made me more nervous, and edgy too.

The pulses stopped after a while, but the energy burst was still there, though lessened a bit. It puzzled me all the more, since the nature of the signal was more like those I'd gotten from suns at great distances.

A little later, well out-system, I perceived the L-jump. It was a big one; Baby Seiglein was taking no chances on Moses, on me, or on not reaching the beacon before his conventional-space fuel ran out.

"They're gone," I sighed, but didn't move to jump

116

us back right away. Something nagged at me, something told me not to go, not to return, to stay, to do anything but return to the Christmas system.

George sensed my hesitation.

"We've got to go, you know," he said softly. "You have to do it, Bar. Come on, let's get it over with."

Finally, that nagging fear still within me, I made the jump.

It took another hour to bring us in-system. I am very conservative in my jumps, always. I don't want to risk even the astronomically small chance of winding up in a sun.

The ship's radiation deflection shields snapped on, a procedure which is automatic but which startled me nonetheless. That shouldn't have happened this far out, I thought, nerves getting worse.

We closed on Patmos, but not too close. I stopped almost fifty thousand kilometers out. But if the sensors weren't broken, I had seen enough.

The radiation count was off the scale for the planet, the surface temperature averaged over 500°C, much hotter in spots. There were no ice caps, nothing. I couldn't test the atmosphere without probing, but the instruments indicated it wouldn't be anything familiar.

I think I screamed. The others rushed up to me, tried to calm me down, tried to control me. I was wild; I resisted, I kicked, I spit webbing, I smashed into things. It took all three and several minutes until I could control myself, and I lay exhausted on the deck.

I thought of them all—Guz, the point, Mara—all gone.

"What happened?" George asked calmly, slowly, soothingly. "Just relax and tell us." I think he already knew the answer. I tried to get my breath; I was sobbing and my chest was heaving madly.

I couldn't speak. George understood, saw my aura,

and said the words for me. "He's killed them all, hasn't he?" he prodded, a sadness that was genuine yet somehow clinical in his tone.

I nodded. "That bastard!" I stopped a minute. "No, George, *I* killed them. *I* brought Seiglein here."

George softened even more, the clinical tone gone.

"No, Bar. They were as good as dead with Moses anyway. You took the only way out. You did the only thing you could. Besides, that was a joint decision— I was in on it, too, remember. We knew the risk, and we took it."

I could only think of that world, of the greenness, the hills, the rushing river—and the billion or more Choz.

"I must say I expected something like this," George continued. "I resigned myself to it. You were blind not to realize what would happen, Bar. If it hadn't been for Eve, here, I might have stopped you, but I couldn't. Not really."

I didn't follow his reasoning. He *knew?* Knew and didn't point it out to me?

"Oh, God! How I hate them!" I spat. "All of them. Any race that could do this, wipe out a whole planet! And they must have planned it ahead of time! They used dirty weapons not seen for centuries! They had to get them out of storage, along with the means of firing them! They must have dropped the whole nuclear bomb stockpile down there! Nothing will ever live on that planet again! We're the last of our race, George! The last!"

"Snap out of it!" the older man bristled sharply. "I've lost far more than you! You have been one of us less than a year, Bar. One Breed, and always in control! I've been one so long I can hardly recall what it's like not being one. Those people down there— many were my own children, my associates! What have you lost except your pride? Except the egomania? Nobody ever beats Bar Holliday! Ha!"

His diatribe was cruel and acidic and was just what

I needed. I struggled to my feet, furious, but, once up and facing him, the two kids staying discreetly back, I calmed down.

This was George, dammitall! George! And he was right.

I looked over at the children. Hell of an exhibition, I thought suddenly. Hell of an example, too. They couldn't understand death, had never faced or experienced it. They had lost nothing but a promise; this ship was *their* world, and we were the only people they'd ever known.

I sighed and relaxed.

"Are you all right?" Eve tried, concerned.

I nodded. "I'm okay now. Don't worry anymore. But don't forget, either! *Never* forget the humans and what they did to our people! *Never* be too big, or too grown, or too civilized to show rage, emotion, *care*." I stopped, feeling the rage building up in me again.

"We all love you, Bar," Ham said softly. "We're one together, all of us."

Love, I thought. Hadn't heard much about that in a long while. Not ever, really. One of George's terms. Humans always equated it with sex. But not George, I thought suddenly. Never George. There was a kinship among us four, I realized, that went beyond the biological. We were a family, and we cared.

"We're not the last, Bar," George said in that earlier, softer tone. "We're the first. Again. Remember what I said about Eve? I knew they'd blow the planet, really. They had to. Our very existence is a threat to them. The virus, Bar. It's not stable. It's programmed to maintain a Patmos condition. All we'd have to do is expose them to us and they'd be exposed to the Patmos condition. They were doctors out to kill an infection. They failed—they got the bulk, but Moses and we are still at large. They'll be back for us both, with full guns blazing, sparing neither manpower nor expense.

"Look—Moses understood. All he had to do was breed a large number of us and land us on some other planets. A passive invasion. No matter what happened to the invaders, the real invaders, the virus, would be loose. It might take years to breed fast enough, but eventually it would take over. Winds, flying things, the very microbes in the air. As fast as humans could find a toxin the virus would change into something slightly different with the same result. You've seen how fast it can stimulate cell growth. Imagine how fast it could breed, the immunity it could develop to almost everything!"

I stopped. I hadn't thought of any of this, really. But George—George was a lot of things, that's why he'd been a master. A biologist by profession, really.

I looked at him. "That means we're flying time bombs for the human race," I said in wonder.

"We sure are," George agreed. "And with Eve approaching maturity, in a few months there'll be more. And still more later. And not all that much later, either!"

That brought another thought to mind.

"George, what's going to happen when breeding starts?" I asked him. "I mean, we can handle maybe a dozen here, no more. This ship should be good for years, but it just doesn't have the room."

"Can we find someplace else?" he suggested. "After all, this is a ship outfitted for that purpose, and you're a scout trained to carry out such a mission."

"The odds! The odds, George!" I protested. "First, not more than one in a hundred systems has planets. Second, no more than one in a thousand has the most basic planets in the right positions. Not more than one in a hundred thousand has the kind of planet we need. It might take fifty years or more to find a good one."

George frowned. "Seems to me that's poor odds. How many scouts are there, anyway?"

"About two hundred," I replied. "About half out at any one time. But, you see, Seiglein's people are equipped to Terraform suitable planets. One in five to ten thousand can be Terraformed, even have an atmosphere added. We have nothing to do that with aboard!"

George considered this. "Sure we do. The best agent there is if the place is anything anybody can work with, has anything organic. Remember how we grew a field out of a small pile of manure? And you've still got lots of those little things in deep-freeze."

The nurds, I thought. Yes, they would carry the infection, and the seed.

"But the problem is, George, that it would still take a lot longer than we've got," I pointed out. "Not only that, but I couldn't use my screens or my spectrometric equipment. We'd be flying blind."

"Then we need to buy more time," George responded. "We have to have the time to breed, the time to look, and the time to try and move things more in our biological favor."

"What do you mean?" I asked, hope rising slightly in me again.

"Well, if you can solve the first problem, somehow, I think, with your help, we might be able to use your computer to solve the second. Remember, you've got an entire biological laboratory here to test out new planets. You're not a biologist—so that computer of yours must know a hell of a lot about it, can do most of it. If Moses can create and program these viruses, then we can, too!"

Nobody beats Bar Holliday. Problems are challenges, and challenges must be met and conquered.

I threw myself into the work. I was a fanatic. The bombing of Patmos had cut whatever cords still bound me to humanity; I was totally an alien now, totally divorced from them, totally dedicated to the revenge that I knew must come.

I considered the most pressing problem first, thinking on it for several cycles. Where could we get extra space, undetected, to breed? Where could we go, what could we find that would serve, at least temporarily? Not a human planet, surely. Those wretches wouldn't be above nuking another one, if that would get the whole batch. And, although they had some planets that we couldn't use, ideal conditions for them approached ideal conditions for us.

In the meantime, I assisted George with the work on the virus, which was strange; I had the computer link, so I had to be the one to arrange everything, yet in many cases I hadn't the slightest idea what was going on. George had forgotten a lot, but he still knew the questions to ask, and the computer, to my surprise, knew the answers. George was right—the computer had all the biological knowledge necessary, better than Moses because it was more up to date.

Our lack of conventional vision was the worst problem. We couldn't view slides or the like. So I worked on that with the computer, trying to rig a system so we could "see" what was going on. What we managed wasn't great, but it would do: a sonic code, that the computer would translate from the dots that made up the pictures. The system wasn't foolproof and it was slow going—since the sound limit gave us a top-to-bottom scan but no stable image—but it worked well enough.

I still hadn't any real idea what we were looking at, but to George it provided the last valuable tool. I had some training in interpreting slides and specimens, enough to do my job. But the bulk of the work on a new planet was always done from the readout of information from the computer when I got back. I had been able to identify the virus in the initial Patmos survey, but would have been unable to combat it or understand its nature.

Not so with George. He was like one of the kids, happy, playful, almost overjoyed at his work. Moreover, Eve showed some interest in what we were doing, so he had a helpful pupil as well. As for me, I followed much of what he was doing, and learned a lot, but it was boring and repetitious work, with little gain from day to day. Had I not been necessary to the job, I would not have been part of it.

And yet, it was I who had the most pressing problem. I had only a year, no more, to develop and execute a plan for some place to expand. I had to assume the worst, that Eve would produce the full six eggs, putting ten of us in the scout ship. We *might* handle ten, but that would be tough and crowded, and the food supply would be iffy. But in a sense they, too, would be time bombs for us—two years to learn, to mature, to grow and become people. Ham and Eve were real people only six months after they were born.

The decision would have to be made by the end of the Breed; we'd have to smash the eggs, or, at best, kill them as soon as they emerged from the pouch.

I could cheerfully have killed Seiglein, or Olag, or any human, but I didn't think I could kill a Choz. I also didn't think, even if we could, that it would be best for the start of a new civilization to found it on murder for expediency. So the problem had to be solved, and quickly. Even a year sounds like a long time, but it would take time to get anyplace.

One thing was sure: the future had to start in the rear, back within the human worlds. If I struck out for unexplored territory, we *might* get lucky, *might* find a place. But the odds were too great, and, once there, we would be too far to turn back. The decision would, in a sense, be forced.

All my life I had resented forced decisions, so I jumped long for the human worlds, trying to find an answer.

What, after all, did we need?

Space—space for a growing population, at least at the start. Not a planet, no. That wouldn't work. And we hadn't the tools or technology to build our own place, nor the hands with which to build them.

And then, one day, heading back, it hit me.

There were, last I knew, a hundred and four human worlds. On a big map, they would be a small group, but distances were deceiving. The closest ones averaged fifty light-years apart, except for the eight that were in paired, multiplanetary systems. The furthest averaged over three hundred and fifty.

It took a lot of commerce to connect those worlds, to supply them with what they lacked from the core factory worlds. Lots of freighters, some almost half as large as the *Peace Victory,* moved regularly among them. They had minimal crews—two to five—and they had open computers.

If we could take one—if, somehow, we could take one—we would solve the immediate problem. But, how did a ship without weapons, a fly speck next to one of the huge freighters, capture it? Especially with two adults, one of whom had never done anything underhanded in his life, and two naive kids? With no hands or weapons except their own bodies against the humans inside?

Fourteen

Ship's sensors showed a long shape approaching—almost two kilometers. I stood there, nervously wishing that there was some way to know what the ships carried. A cargo of robots or an automated machine shop would be very handy; a billion synthetic steaks or spare parts for Creatovisions would be worse than useless.

"This one?" Ham asked, nervous but excited.

I studied the scene. "No," I responded. "It would be nice to take it, but a ship that big has to have a crew of five or so, maybe even a passenger section. We can't afford that."

Reluctantly, we let the long little world we needed coast on by and watched it braking for docking orbit off a new and nameless planet that was still being Terraformed.

I chose this area because it would have the most traffic and the least military. Not that the military was very large—there were no more than three ships the size of *Courrant*, and perhaps two hundred or so smaller vessels. There was no need for a large force, since there was social stability. The people as a whole were so vegetative that they would revolt only if the system broke down completely. The creative ones, the bright-eyed kids raised by the corporations and the state, were, for the most part, turned into dull, plodding, unimaginative cogs in the corporate system. The system ate minds, consumed them, but while it was dull and stagnant it was not threatened.

In fact, the military's major employment was in large-scale construction projects; it existed only because a power structure never quite feels comfortable without one, and because of the theoretical threat of an extraterrestrial, nonhuman civilization that might be found someday, but which had never materialized.

Until now.

Now, the four who posed that threat sat in a tiny spacecraft hidden by some of the natural debris always floating around near a solar system, waiting to pounce.

Several hours passed, but, the Choz have infinite patience and a poor time sense.

Another ship showed—still too big, too formidable-looking.

Finally one came along that met our specifications, but it was followed too closely by another. Timing was everything here; the emergence point from the L-jump was, as is standard with babies this size, quite a distance from the target solar system. Out of range of the routine system sensors, really. We needed one, alone, with no other ship in the vicinity that could pick up calls.

Seven more passed and were rejected as time went.

Finally, the traffic eased up. Obviously a large shipment was going in; this had been some sort of a convoy.

We waited patiently, knowing that we could afford no mistakes, knowing that a ship would eventually come that was right. And one did—a smaller ship, less than a kilometer but nice and wide, like a great, fat arrow.

"This is it," I warned the others. "Places!"

I kicked in the automated distress call on my ship, using less than a third strength. This had the advantage of reducing the risk of others hearing it. Or making it seem like my power was down to those who did hear it.

The freighter heard it. It started to slow; I could see the energy brakes come on.

"This is the *Nijinsky* calling ship in distress," came a female voice. "Come in, ship in distress."

"This is Seiglein Scout 3167," I replied through the computer, using a number just a little higher than the corporation was now using. "I am just back from sector scouting and I have had an accident."

Silence for a moment, then she asked, "All right, Seiglein 3167. Have you any motive power? Can you make it to our lock?"

"I believe so," I responded. "I was injured in the crash, though. Do you have a doctor aboard?"

"Negative on the doctor. We are a freighter, and there are only two of us aboard. However, we can administer first-aid until we get you to the medical station on Loki . . . We are homing on your signal. Maintain your present heading."

Luck was running with us; I'd judged the ship and crew exactly. As important as the ship itself was the fuel it held; my little ship used only a small bit for in-system work, and had a reserve, but it could tap the fuel supply of the big one without restricting the *Nijinsky*'s capabilities very much. Like taking an eyedropper's worth from a billion-liter tank.

They closed rapidly and soon locked on.

"I'm too hurt to move through the lock," I told them. "You will have to come and get me."

"We're on automatic now," *Nijinsky* replied. "Coming aft."

We lowered the lights to minimum; we didn't need them, anyway, and kept them on only for the plants; you couldn't turn off the upper deck and leave the lowers on. To the humans, it would be almost total darkness.

George was positioned against the wall near the air lock; I was pressed against the wall facing the lock, but quite a bit back. We had practiced this maneuver several times on each other but there was a strong undercurrent of nervousness now that the real thing was upon us.

Ham and Eve held back; they couldn't spin web yet, so they waited in case we missed or things went wrong. Then they would have to move fast to save us. I was counting on the total lack of aggression in human society; there being no threat, they would be expecting nothing untoward now.

The lock opened, and I could see two figures hesitate, then start through. The dummies weren't wearing spacesuits!

"Jesus! His power's gone. It's dark in there," warned the first figure, the woman I'd spoken with on the radio. "Watch your step!"

"Right behind you, Marsha," responded another, also a female voice.

When the first one was inside, we waited, motionless, for the second to come through. Since we could talk in frequencies they couldn't hear, I gave running instructions: "George, get the second one as soon as she clears. Ham, Eve—I don't see any weapons, but be ready. On my signal . . . *Now!*"

"Hey! Scout! Where are—" the one called Marsha started to shout, then George's webbing struck the second woman, wrapping around her arms, while my own did the same for Marsha.

They yelled and struggled, and we cut the web and started again, lower down.

The other one turned and started to run but George wrapped web around her feet and she fell with a crash on the deck, continuing to struggle.

Marsha turned, too, and I missed on my first try at her legs, but in her panic she struck the other woman and started over. I shot webbing back and forth, binding them on the deck in an awkward position, almost on top of one another.

They struggled against their bonds, but could do nothing.

I hooked into the vocal circuits of the computer.

"Don't struggle anymore," I warned them, affecting as soothing a tone as I could. "You will not be harmed if you behave."

Both calmed down a little, but then I had to jump over them to get into *Nijinsky* and was briefly silhouetted by the light from the freighter.

One woman screamed. "My God! They—they're monsters!" she yelled. I had no time for her hysteria. I raced for the *Nijinsky*'s bridge, imagining all sorts of ships closing in on us, discovering us before we could move.

I made the bridge in record time, much faster than a human could run, and took a quick scan. Everything was on standby.

Nervously I fumbled with the switches I knew would open the computer system. Suddenly, I was conscious of time for the first time in a long while. Trying to do what I had to quickly, with hooves not designed for it, I missed the proper switches again and again. Finally, I calmed myself and thought out my actions, then got the sequence right.

I could feel the computer link cut in: a primitive model—ship's functions, navigation, the jump math, little more. It was enough. I enlarged the energy field to cover my ship, a relatively simple affair, then matched velocities as best I could, hopefully for a ten-hour jump. Then, with a silent prayer that all were braced for the inevitable as they had been warned, I made the jump.

As ship's sensors blanked and the bang threw me away from the control panel—in my excitement *I'd* forgotten to brace—I felt a wave of relief and exultation.

We'd done it!

Battered and bruised though I was, I was in no mood to feel pain. I disregarded it, sensing no broken bones and knowing that the body would immediately begin self-repair.

My concern had been fuel. However, the registers

showed over two-thirds full. No real problem there.

After a few minutes to catch my breath, I adjusted the internal temperature and humidity more to our liking and made my way, more slowly now, back to my own ship. As I went, I reflected that I had run the distance along narrow corridors, catwalks, and the like, some strewn with metal obstacles.

I knew that a human couldn't have made that run without tripping and breaking his neck. Choz vision was definitely superior for this sort of thing. I was still amazed at how easy the whole thing had been. Incredibly so. Maybe I was a born pirate, I thought. A pirate certainly could do a nice piece of work in an age that didn't believe in pirates.

And, if we were lucky, if no one had seen any part of it, there was a good chance that no one would ever know what happened. There were always mechanical breakdowns of one sort or another; rarely did they result in the loss of a ship, but such things *did* happen.

I went back to the air lock. The two women were still trapped in the webbing. One was breathing hard, nervously. The other was sobbing softly, and she gave a low, frightened groan when I leaped over them into the bridge of my own ship.

I quickly adjusted my computer to the settings of the *Nijinsky* so there would be no accidents, and adjusted the energy field so that it, too, matched that of the larger ship.

George was there, looking strangely at our two prisoners. Ham and Eve were nearby, too, quietly surveying the strange beings trapped on the deck. These were the first humans they'd ever seen.

"How are things?" I asked.

"All right, I suppose," George responded slowly, still looking at the two women. "They screamed and struggled for some time before settling down to what you see."

I looked at him intently. "What's the matter, George? We did it!"

He nodded. "Yes, we did it. Somehow—well, it had to be done, and I'm glad it was done well, smoothly. Even so, I had let myself forget that we would be trapping innocent people, forcing them into captivity."

"But, they're humans, George!" I protested. "They're the enemy!"

He shook his head sadly. "No, Bar, not the enemy. The *system's* the enemy, not the individuals."

I glanced over at the women. "Okay, we'll drop them at a beacon somewhere. That make you happy?"

His hue projected sadness, but reflected sympathy. "You know we can't do that, Bar. It would be even worse for them, and worse for us. They'd starve, Bar, or undergo the Change and tip off the government that we're about. They're infected now. Already the virus has touched them, through our air, through the webbing. Already it is duplicating, doubling and doubling again, forcing out the stuff it replaces. See the golden mist about them, even through the flight suits? That's the water carrying the fluids and molecules out through the pores as the virus dominates their cells. Within hours, no more, they'll be as biologically nonhuman as we. Put them downstairs and they'll start to eat, start to change into us. It's in the programming of the virus."

He was right, of course, as usual. The only problem I could see with it, though, was the chance that they would go mad. The only hope that I had was that they were either more stable personalities than we had a right to expect, or that they were so immunized by Creatovision that they'd simply accept it as they would a new programming idea.

I adjusted the computer for lower register speech.

"All right, all right, take it easy," I soothed as best I could, wishing I could tie George into the computer. How often I'd wished that! "Just relax and I'll explain what this is all about."

There was a muffled sob from one, I couldn't tell which, but the one I'd talked to initially spoke, terri-

131

fied, upset, nervous—but not mad. It was a good sign.

"Who—what—are you?" she gasped.

"We are the Choz," I responded. "And, yes, you're right, we are not human."

"What happened to the scout who originally flew this ship?" she asked, the question doubling as an invitation to tell her her own fate.

"I am the pilot, the original one," I responded. "Once I was as human as you are. As I became one of them, not through choice although now I prefer it, so will you."

"I won't become a monster!" the other one screamed. Bad sign. She might be trouble.

I sighed, choosing my words carefully.

"There was a world called Patmos," I began, and then told them the story, or rather, the story as George and I had told it to Ham and Eve.

"The virus is in you now," I concluded. "There's no way to stop it. Let it run its course. Don't resist. Believe me, this existence is not at all bad or unpleasant. It's just different. We're sorry we had to involve you, but we had no choice. They have destroyed our world, made it unfit for life. We are the last."

"Turn up the lights," Marsha asked. "Let us see what you look like."

"Monsters!" the other murmured.

I turned the lights up slowly.

"Monsters, yes, I suppose, by human definition. But you must forget human definitions now. The navy forced us to this, human action forced us to trap you."

Although the light meant nothing to me, it did allow the colors to come into sharp relief.

I heard Marsha gasp as she saw me.

"Oh, my God!" she gasped. "You were *never* human!"

I attempted a shrug. The Choz gesture was meaningless to them.

"You'll see. You have three choices, and only three. I will honor whichever of the three you want. First, you can accept the situation, go through the Change which is already starting within you, cast your lot in with us. Because of the virus within you—and now throughout both ships, in the atmosphere—you can never return to your past lives."

"And the other choices, then?" Marsha prompted.

"You can choose to die," I responded as emotionlessly as I could. "The Choz don't die. The virus can repair almost any damage, fight every infection, make new cells that are as good as the original to replace the old. I suppose we'll die someday, when our brain cells go, but that could be a long, long time. But, right now, we could kill you, we could flush you out into space as soon as we come out of the jump."

"Let us go!" the other pleaded. "Drop us at a beacon! The Corporation will find a cure for us!"

"Which one did you work for?" I asked sharply.

"Seiglein," they both answered, making it a sort of litany. Their faith in my old employer was somehow sadly touching.

"So did I," I told them. "This is a Seiglein ship. It was Jerry Seiglein himself who tried to kill us, almost certainly blew up the beacon that I used, and destroyed our planet. No, citizens, it's easier for them to kill you than to cure you—if they could, which I doubt."

"You said there were three choices," Marsha said. "What is the third?"

"You can resist, refuse to accept what happened, and go mad," I replied.

They were silent for a minute, mulling over what I'd just told them. The one, Marsha, seemed to be pretty stable. She might make it. The other—well, I didn't know about her.

Finally, Marsha asked, "Can we be released? Can we get somewhere and think about this?"

The computer symbolically cleared its throat, reflecting my unease.

"I'm afraid that dissolving the webbing is—ah, a

messy chore, and one that must wait on circumstances. We'll release you as soon as we can." I turned to the others, waiting expectantly, not knowing how to act or what to do, unable, at the moment, to join in the conversation although able to listen to it.

"Ask them about themselves," Eve prompted. "We should know something about them. Wow! They look so *weird,* so strange! I never thought humans would look like that—so little, so soft, so weak."

I chuckled. First impressions from a one-hundred-percent alien creature.

"Ham?" I prompted. "Any comments?"

"If that's what humans are like," he replied firmly, "praise God I'm a Choz!"

"George?"

"May as well do what Eve says," the biologist responded. "After all, they may well be part of the family soon. Besides, they have a big advantage over us—they're younger, I think, and they *know* what's happening and what's going to happen, even if they haven't accepted it yet."

I nodded. "Look, while we wait, tell us about yourselves. You—your name is Marsha? Mine is Bar Holliday. The others here, who cannot now speak with you, are George Haspinol and our two children, Ham and Eve."

"Why can't they talk?" Marsha asked apprehensively.

"Choz speech is ultra-high-frequency audio, beyond the range of human hearing," I explained. "Don't worry, you'll hear them later."

"So that's why your voice sounds so strange and disembodied!" Marsha exclaimed. "I'm really talking to the ship's computer!"

"To me through the computer," I acknowledged. "For now, anyway."

They were silent, then the other one said, so softly it was hard to be heard, "This isn't happening. This does not happen. Not to people, not to anybody, most of all not to me."

I ignored her. "So who are you, Marsha?"

"Marsha 47-3856-27 Vonderhall," she said. "I'm twenty, and I qualified as a ship's pilot only eight months ago." I nodded. That fit. The milk runs were the first commands assigned to new graduates.

I introduced myself again, and gave her some of my background. That seemed to have a soothing effect simply because she was hearing something familiar.

"And you," I said, addressing the other one. "Who are you?"

"I don't have to tell you nothin'," she responded.

"You don't indeed," I admitted, "but a name at least would be helpful. It's a lot better than 'Citizen' or 'Hey! You!'"

"Oh, shit, this isn't happening anyway," she said, more to herself than to me. "Nadya. Nadya 38-7632-01 Yamato."

"Okay, Nadya, I think I can free you both now. I warn you, though, that we have more webbing, that it's almost impossible for you to overpower us or hurt us much, and that you'd better do as we say or elect to be dumped."

They both nodded, still scared. When I explained how I was going to dissolve the webbing, they were even more upset. I didn't blame them; I didn't much like getting pissed on, either.

"Bar!" George said suddenly. "This may be what we're waiting for! I just thought of it! Marvelous! They'll have to be downstairs anyway, near the food. We can take samples, Bar! Samples as things go along! Watch how the virus works, its patterns, what molecule chain does what! Their change might give us the key!"

I nodded. George's basic problem was that he had been working with stable samples. The virus was a normal part of our and the plant's cellular structures. Now we could see it operating in high gear.

I finished, and was putting up with nasty comments from the two women as well as with their overall revulsion. But I'd gotten the bulk of the webbing; the rest was mostly covering their one-piece jumpsuits, which were soon going to be superfluous anyway.

"Look," I explained to them as they slowly rose, trying to wipe away the sticky stuff, "George is a biologist. We are trying to solve the riddle of this virus, to control it. You can help, if you will." I was trying to remember the sequence of my own Change.

"God! I'm starving!" Nadya exclaimed suddenly.

I nodded. The Change was starting.

Let's see, I thought. First day was the internal change in the digestive system. Well and good. Second day some external changes, the hair, longer arms. Only by the third day did the hands become useless.

For the first two days they would be able to do something we couldn't—manage a syringe, take blood samples that involved more than just cutting yourself and wiping it on a slide.

"Move down the ramp," I ordered them, trying to keep my tone normal, conversational, slightly friendly. They looked around at us—we were standing there, poised and ready, with huge muscles and tough skin— and complied. Ham and Eve preceded them, George and I followed.

Marsha gasped as she saw the main lounge. The whole floor was a jungle of tall grass, the fixtures, old furniture, and lab stuff rising incongruously out of it.

"We're herbivores, plant-eaters," I told them, and this information seemed to reassure Nadya a little. I considered it—frankly, in their position I might have thought about being eaten, too. "This little garden is our food supply."

"Can't we get some chops from our ship, then?" Nadya pleaded. "I'm starving!"

Marsha said nothing, but the mention of food produced an unconscious reaction in her.

"Look down in the grass, at the base of the blades,"

I told them. They bent down and looked curiously at the tubers. "Try one," I suggested. "You'll find they aren't bad at all."

"I'm not going to eat your alien stuff!" the older woman protested. "It might poison me! We have plenty of food in our ship."

"Eat the tubers or starve," I said flatly. "It's the quickest way."

"To what?" Marsha asked nervously.

I sighed. "You know for what."

They thought for a while, and sat down in the grass. Marsha cut herself on the sharp blades.

"Watch the cuts," I told her. "Just keep watching them."

She looked puzzled, but did as she was told. I knew what she was seeing, too. The blood stopped, then a scab formed, almost visibly.

"It's healing over!" she breathed. "The sting's gone!"

"See?" I said. "You're already on the way."

They just sat there for a while, Marsha staring at her cuts, Nadya looking uneasily around the lounge.

"Smells like shit in here," the older woman said.

I shrugged. "What do you think fertilizes plants?" I responded lightly. "You'll get used to it."

We were looking over slides and checking things out sometime later; Ham and Eve were idly grazing, keeping watch on the two prisoners, whose hunger was growing by the hour. Still, they resisted the tubers—and that took willpower, I knew.

"I might as well go over to the *Nijinsky* and scout it out," I said to George. I turned to the two women. "Either of you know your cargo manifest?"

"A little of everything," Marsha responded. "Why not read it yourself?"

I turned and faced her. "Look at my eyes. See?"

She'd been looking at all our eyes for some time, but they must have seemed like a disguise, I suppose.

We were so strange-looking that they hadn't considered the minor details.

"You're blind!" she gasped. "But then—how . . . ?"

I shook my head. "Not blind. We just see differently, by sound rather than light waves. Your system is better for humans, ours better for Choz. The more I use it, the better I like it."

I turned and was partway up the ramp when Eve screamed.

"George! Watch out! She's going to—"

I whirled, and saw Nadya pick up something, probably a piece of the smashed sample panel, and rush at George, whose back was turned toward the bioscreen.

George whirled and suddenly I experienced something I'd never experienced before as man or Choz.

Vision blurred, there was a tremendous, high-pitched screech, the sound waves so penetrating that they made the whole lounge look like a mass of crackling electricity.

I adjusted to it quickly, editing it down so that my own frequency worked around the all-encompassing one. It produced a strange sort of vision—the lounge, the humans and Choz in it in strange outline beneath a fiery haze. The sound—the sound was coming from George, from George and from Ham! They were staring hard at Nadya, who seemed frozen, mouth open in shock and surprise, a statue—hand raised, a nasty piece of plastic still in her hand, poised to strike.

And I saw she *was* moving, but slowly, so slowly that you could hardly see it. The whole room seemed to be operating in slow motion, except for George, who sidestepped.

Marsha, still sitting in the grass, had just begun turning, a puzzled expression on her face, and was starting to bring her hands up to her ears, mouth open. It would take her some time to do that.

Suddenly Ham jumped, knocking Nadya down in

real time. The piece of plastic flew from her still outstretched hand. Eve saw it and stepped on it, not once, but again and again, until it was ground up into little pieces.

And then, just as suddenly, the sound diminished by half, then left entirely.

The two humans reverted to normal speed as well. Nadya, sprawled and bleeding from Ham's kick, completed the downstroke of her outstretched hand, while Marsha, hands over her ears, snapped her head around.

To say that I was stunned was an understatement. And, as interesting as my own shock and those of the two women, was the bewilderment on the part of George, Ham, and Eve.

"I'll be damned!" I managed.

"Probably," George responded drily. "Now what in the world caused *that?*"

"That incredible sound wave," I managed, "it came from you—and from Ham. How'd you *do* that?"

George seemed genuinely puzzled. "I haven't the slightest idea. I heard Eve cry out, turned, and saw the woman coming for me. Then she just seemed to slow down, and my vision blurred for an instant."

"You must have had to clear Ham's signal," I noted. "If you saw her slow down you didn't even realize your whatever-it-was was on."

George nodded. "Ham? Do you know how we did what we just did?"

Ham was busy picking himself up, and he exhibited an angry hue. He glared at the wounded, groaning woman.

"Humans!" he spat. "All alike!" Suddenly hearing George, he seemed to snap out of it. His tone softened, changed. "No, I don't know what happened. I just—well, I heard Eve, and then the whole place exploded. As soon as my vision came back I went for her."

The Web of the Chozen

"Sound waves," George mused, "can do all sorts of things. Break glass, tumble big buildings, given the right intensity and pitch. This one seems to paralyze the human nervous system, but not ours. Fascinating."

I frowned. "So how come we never heard it before?" I asked. "I still can't imagine how you did it, let alone do it myself."

"It's got to be a defensive weapon," the biologist replied. "We never had anything to defend against before. It's obviously automatic, a reflex action. And it's specifically keyed to humans! Well, well!"

I considered for a moment. "Sure!" I said excitedly, mind racing. "Old Moses was going to drop some of us on human worlds. He was a religious machine, remember. He didn't want to kill people! So he built in passive defense mechanisms!"

"I wonder how many?" George mused. "I wonder if we really *do* know ourselves?"

"We're not defenseless, anyway," I pointed out with some satisfaction. "That alone makes me feel a lot better and more confident."

He nodded, and looked at Nadya. She was still sprawled out, sobbing now. The blood had already dried, but she had broken several bones, that was clear. Ham had spared nothing in his jump.

I sighed, and looked at Marsha, who still seemed stunned, frozen. She was only now taking her hands from her ears, looking scared and bewildered.

I patched into the computer, realizing that she hadn't heard a word of our conversation. To her, the action had been just another manifestation of our alien power. She couldn't know it stunned us as much as them.

"Marsha?" I called to her. At first she didn't answer. "Marsha!" I called again, sharper.

She started, and shook her head slowly up and down.

"Are you all right?" I asked her.

Again the nod; the expression, as near as I could read it, was still blank.

"We had to do that," I said as gently as I could. "I'm sorry." And I *was* sorry, genuinely sorry.

"Why did she do it?" Marsha asked me, blindly bewildered. "What could she have been thinking of?" She turned slowly to Nadya, still groaning nearby. "Why?" she said.

"Monsters!" Nadya sobbed. "They'll eat us when we're fattened! We have to kill the monsters." The last was in such a matter-of-fact tone that it chilled all of us, Marsha included.

"She's mad," George said, and I had to agree.

"Web her down," I ordered the biologist. "This shouldn't happen again."

George complied, practically wrapping the woman in a silvery cocoon as Marsha watched with a mixture or horror and fascination.

George finished quickly; it wasn't an artistic job, but it was thorough. He glanced at Marsha. "What about her?" he asked.

I sighed, thinking a bit. "Marsha?" I called hesitantly. Since the voice came from above and George and I looked alike to her, I realized she didn't know which was me.

"On the ramp," I said. She turned and looked at me, saying nothing.

I considered my speech carefully. "Nadya's made her choice. I'm sorry about it, but there it is. What is yours?"

She still looked to be in shock, but she was thinking now.

"I—I don't want what you offer," she began, and my heart sank, "but—but I don't want to die, Bar Holliday. I don't want to die now."

I exhaled audibly, feeling a little better.

"Then join us," I invited. "It is not really so terrible. It isn't. In many ways it's beautiful."

"I'll try," she managed.

The Web of the Chozen

We emerged from the L-jump on schedule, and I still hadn't made a survey of the *Nijinsky*. Marsha was recovering a bit, but she still refused to eat, even though I knew that hunger must be obsessing her. It's natural to put off the inevitable as long as possible.

I scanned the neighborhood we were in. It took a moment while the computer matched location and quadrant. The freighter didn't have those things in its memory; it knew only the right routes, and the beacon stations. My own computer, however, placed us as still within known space, but well outside any lines of trade or commerce. There were no settled planets this far out, and it was three light-years to the nearest beacon. I could barely detect its wail.

I was satisfied. This was good enough for now. Nobody would be likely to stumble across us, and there were no solar systems in the area to make me use a lot of fuel in the next jump. We had travel options.

One option we didn't have was Nadya.

She was completely gone, mad as they come, gibbering and foaming and screaming about monsters and being eaten.

It took some trouble to figure out how to move her. Finally we managed to turn and web until she was rollable, then we pushed her, with great difficulty, up the ramp, positioned her and tugged her back into the *Nijinsky*. George kept watch over Marsha; Ham and Eve assisted with the nasty task. I didn't like doing it, but I didn't trust Eve alone with Marsha; and I didn't trust Ham not to do something drastic.

"We should do this to the other one, too," he grunted as he pushed and maneuvered the unfortunate madwoman. "No humans should be allowed to join us. Even as Choz they're still human underneath."

"Easy with that talk!" I cautioned him. "Would you dump me out the refuse hatch, too? I started out the same way, remember."

He looked startled. When your whole world was

two decks of a ship and four people, you didn't include them in your pet theories about outsiders.

"Oh, Lord! Of course not, Bar! You're different!"

"No I'm not," I told him. "I'm just like her, only a little more experienced, a little better trained. It's never the outside that counts, Ham, it's the inside."

Eve glared at Ham. "See?" she taunted. "You never think! That's your whole trouble! Besides, remember! If she doesn't work out . . ."

She left it hanging, but she'd said it.

Marsha was on probation. As an outsider, she wasn't like one of our own children, really. She could be taken by us at any time, dumped at any time. I hoped not—this job was unpleasant as it was, and I was beginning to like the woman. She had that little spark that differentiated her from the herd that Nadya and the others belonged to. She was still capable of thought, of adaptation to new circumstances.

And she was a trained pilot, with skills we needed.

We did the deed, not without a lot of reservations and a little guilt on my part. But she was better off out there, dead, gone; gone, if George was right, to some better place. No longer suffering, in any event.

Ham and Eve wanted to explore the new place—it was hundreds of times bigger than anything they'd ever seen or experienced. I told them they could, but only together, and cautioned them against the catwalks and long drops and warned them not to interfere with the cargo. I would be back to join them in a little bit.

I went back to the ship. Marsha was still there, holding her head in her hands. George grazed, watching her idly.

"Has she eaten yet?" I asked him.

"No," he replied. "And look at her—how thin she's getting! You can sound some of the bone structure! The Change is working with what it has, and that isn't enough. If she doesn't eat soon she'll be dead of starvation."

"Marsha?" I said gently. She looked up at me. "You've got to eat something. Try the tubers. They aren't bad. If you don't, you'll kill yourself."

"Nadya . . ." she said hesitantly "She's—she's gone?"

"Yes," I replied sadly. "It had to be, Marsha. And you have to eat. You must."

"She took a blood sample for me," George put in. "I managed to grab a syringe box in my mouth and gave it to her. She got the idea."

I nodded. "Good. If only she'd start! This is getting to me!"

"She's had a bad time all around," George pointed out. "Lord! What willpower she must have!"

"We could use it," I said. "I'd hate to see it go out the waste chute." I hooked into the computer again.

"Marsha, come on!" I prodded. "Suicide's not in your makeup! I can tell that!"

She was quiet a minute, then looked up at me again.

"The smaller green one—the one with the straight horns. That's a female?"

I nodded. "My daughter, Eve."

"I'll—I'll look like her?" she asked hesitantly.

"Sort of," I replied.

"It's all so unreal, like some Creatovision horror!" she exclaimed. "I can't believe it."

"Did you know Nadya long?" I asked.

"No, not at all. We didn't really get along. She was twenty years senior and you knew it every moment."

"That's what you'd have turned into, after a while," I pointed out. "Milk runs, back and forth, the better runs, the bigger rewards, the gold stars on the company chart. Dull, monotonous. You'd have killed yourself or dulled your mind to her level. Now you have a chance, a way out. A chance to be in on something new, something exciting. Join us, woman! Don't kill yourself now!"

She reached down and picked up a tuber, looking at

it oddly. She turned it over and over, peeled back the thin, dark skin.

"Oh, God! I'm so hungry!" she wailed, and she bit into it.

Once started, as I remembered all too well, you were committed. She had held out a long time; maybe I would have, too, if I'd known beforehand what it would do to me.

I watched, amazed, at the transformation in her. No, not the physical one—that was only beginning. It was the raw animalism in her, the sudden, frantic pulling up of the tubers, the sloppy, almost manic way she stuffed them into her mouth and swallowed, only half chewing. I wondered what kept her from choking to death, but, though she coughed many times in the process that didn't happen.

Finally, she reached her limit, that point at which the stuff was practically running out of your mouth. She lay back then, breathing hard, totally exhausted. She'd been terribly weakened by her holdout, and I was concerned for her.

She gave a sudden, long sigh and went limp, breathing more shallowly.

George nodded, and went over to his workbench. "She's on the way now," he said cheerfully. "Want to give me a hand with the blood sample?"

"Later," I told him. "I want to gather up Ham and Eve and see what we have on our prize ship. First things first."

I entered the *Nijinsky* and called out to the kids.

Getting no reply, I started to worry, and moved on down the corridor slowly, toward the bridge. Every few paces I'd call out.

Finally I heard Eve's voice answer my call.

"Bar! Come quick! You'll never believe what we found!"

Fifteen

I was somewhat apprehensive as I made my way toward Eve, cursing myself for leaving them alone in a strange environment, imagining all sorts of dire disasters the two curious kids could get into. It was hard to remember how young and how inexperienced they were.

I rounded a corner but still couldn't see them.

"Down here!" she called, and I found a narrow and fairly difficult ramp twisting down. I did a quick scan of the bottom, but could tell nothing. Just rampway, really.

Almost breaking my neck getting down, I made it to the bottom and saw them. They were just sitting, staring into a large, open doorway.

"I thought I told you not to go into the cargo bays," I scolded.

Ham shrugged. "So? What are cargo bays?"

Feeling outfoxed and foolish, I went up to see what they were looking at so intently.

It was a garden.

No, more accurately, it was a cargo bay, circular, about two hundred meters across.

The floor was a teeming jungle; none of it reflected the food color, but there were vegetative colors galore, a riot of them. Flowers—lots of flowers and shrubs and small trees, in rich, moist soil.

I just stared.

"Is this *their* food garden?" Eve asked innocently. I

thought of the plastic cubes that the robokitchens served up for food on L-ships and chuckled.

"No," I replied. "Not hardly. More likely a hothouse for use in testing areas of the new planet to see what will grow best where. It's an incredible stroke of luck, though—it'll serve us well."

Ham shook his head. "I think it's food for the big animals."

I whirled on him. "What big animals? Where?" I demanded.

He was somewhat taken aback by the vehemence of my response, brought about more by fear than anything else. Animal seeding was not unknown in certain circumstances, and not all of the creatures were nice.

"There," they both responded in unison, gesturing with pointer beams of sound.

I followed the beams, and almost stepped back a bit.

There were two of them. They looked like spiders— huge spiders, with round bodies almost perfectly smooth and eight long, looping legs, tentacles really.

And they were five meters across if they were a milimeter. I'd missed them in the first scan—one had still been on the ground, the other clinging high overhead.

And they had no color or aura, so they were hidden by the growths.

No color or aura, I thought suddenly. Then they weren't organic.

That suited me; I had not wanted to believe in five-meter-wide spiders, let alone share a ship with them.

"They're robots," I told the kids. "See? No color."

"What's a robot?" Eve asked.

"A mechanical creature. Like the ship's computers, only smaller, built by men to do work they didn't want to do or couldn't do themselves."

"You mean built like the virus is building the woman?" Ham asked, curious.

I shook my head. "No, not really. They aren't people. Not life, really. They're machines—like this spaceship."

"They move," Eve insisted. "They are more like us than the ship. Do you mean they can't think?"

I considered this. "I don't know. They're obviously gardeners, programmed to care for this place. They may be able to think, at least a little. Maybe talk, although they don't look like it."

"They've ignored us," Ham pointed out.

I nodded. "That probably means they're programmed only for the garden itself. Let's see if they notice me now. Stand back!" Carefully I stepped over the ledge, stopping as soon as my tail cleared the hatch.

The one overhead noticed me all right. It whirled, twirled, and, faster than I'd have believed possible, moved over close to me. It stood there, on the ceiling, pulsating slowly up and down on its legs, and, although I could detect no head or sensory apparatus as such, I knew it was looking at me. I stood dead still.

It was a crazy tableau, and I knew prolonging it would gain nothing. The thing could wait longer than I could.

"Robot!" I called out, hoping it could receive the high-frequency content of my voice. "Robot, do you hear me?"

The thing barely twitched, but I could feel something looking me over suspiciously, like a slightly warm ray of the sun.

"Insect, insect, insect in garden," it suddenly said in a sizzling electronic monotone.

"No! Not insect!" I called back at it, but it reared back and let fly with the foulest-smelling spray I could remember ever breathing. It was sticky, and wet, and unpleasant, and it came at me as a lead-colored fog.

I moved fast, whirling and jumping for the door. I felt a cold tentacle strike me hard on the back, and I cried out in pain; now it had hold of my hind legs, and I struggled for the door. Ham and Eve, alarmed, moved just inside.

"No!" I screamed. "Stay back!"

Suddenly I felt the grip loosen. "Swarm! Swarm!" said the robot, and I leaped painfully for the open hatch and made it. Eve turned to follow me, Ham covering the rear.

Then, suddenly, it was back again—that high-pitched, awful screech of the Choz sonic defense mechanism.

Checking to see that Eve got out, I nursed bruised legs and a nasty welt on my back and looked at the scene inside.

"Ham!" I yelled. "Get out of there if you can!"

The sound had confused the robot. It stopped, and whirled around, the screech's echo doubling against the walls of the garden. The other robot, which up to now had played no part in the drama, also reacted, trying first to come to the aid of its partner, then, like it, whirling in confusion.

I made it to the hatchway, knowing that Ham was safe as long as he continued the tone, but would be nabbed the moment he turned to run. I didn't know what to do or how to do it. Tension and fear for him welled up inside of me, and, suddenly, I too was broadcasting the tone into the garden.

The robots stopped, whirled, changed position to meet this new threat, which was as puzzling as the first. Ham didn't need any cues—he turned and almost landed on top of me in one giant leap.

Just as suddenly the tone disappeared.

The robots continued to whirl for a few moments, then slowed, moving first a little one way, then another, in a confused, almost dazed manner. It was clear what had happened; they had faced a phenomenon that their programming wasn't prepared for.

"Bridge! Bridge!" I heard them call. "Bridge! Bridge!"

"Come on!" I called to the kids, and we moved forward, toward the bridge area. It was extremely painful for me, and that sticky feeling and terrible odor were all-pervasive, but I made it.

The Web of the Chozen

Entering the bridge, I heard what I'd hoped to hear. The tinny, voices of the two robots calling the bridge.

Quickly I located an intercom, hoping still that my voice wasn't outside the range of transmission or reception.

With great difficulty, I turned the little lever, linking the bridge with the transceiver in the robots.

"This is the bridge," I said as calmly as I could. Actually, I was out of breath, panting, tongue hanging.

There was a sudden silence at the other end. They had received at least the carrier, some kind of response.

"Gardeners 41 and 42 in Hold K," came the robot's monotone. "We have been infested with large insects beyond our capability to handle. They are now loose within the ship. We suggest an immediate search and fumigation under Section XXIV, title 6, subsection 3a of the Interplanetary Convention Health Codes, and stand by to assist."

"Negative, Gardeners 41 and 42," I responded with as much intensity as I could manage. "Negative. Do you read?"

There was silence for a moment, then they repeated their message.

Clearly, the transmission equipment just wasn't up to carrying sounds in the forty-thousand-plus-cycles-per-second range. Frantically, I looked around the control room. The kids stood back, not knowing what to do. I cursed the fact that I couldn't use my own ship's computer voice to transmit to the local intercom.

And then, suddenly, I stopped short. Maybe I could. I turned to the kids.

"Look, children, you stay here," I ordered crisply. "The radio reception circuitry is still on here. Here! Ham! Come over here!"

He came over to the panel.

"See that knob?" I said, using a sound pointer. He nodded. "Well, if you turn it to the right it increases the volume; to the left, it decreases. I'm going back to

150

the scout and I'll call through here on the radio. I want you to turn that knob so that my voice is as loud as you can make it and still understand me. Okay?"

"Sure," he replied. "It's got some ridges. I think I can turn it with my hoof."

I nodded. "Okay, then. Listen for me." I turned to Eve. "Now, girl, you stand by the intercom, here. When I tell you, you turn this switch like this. See?" I demonstrated and she nodded understanding. I turned back to Ham. "Now, when I tell you, you throw that lever, there. That will put you into an open circuit. I won't be able to hear you over this damned human-designed system, but I should be able to pick up the intercom, barely, at that volume. You stay still, both of you, or your own sounds will interfere. Any trouble, knock the panel three times and we'll come running."

Satisfied, I went back to the scout. My wounds from the gardener robot were really painful and I was starting to feel stiff; I needed a good sleep's repair, but I didn't have time for it now. I was too excited.

I made it into the bridge of my own ship and patched quickly into the computer.

"Okay, Ham," I said through the radio. "I'll start counting, and keep counting until you tap the panel twice. That will tell me you're at maximum loudness."

I started counting, slowly, and as I did I started to hear sounds coming back a little, some distortion and feedback from being so close. Finally, at thirty-one, Ham tapped twice.

"Good," I told him. "Now, Eve, you throw that switch at the same time Ham throws the lever on his panel. Don't worry—I'll know when it's open. Then stay as still as you can."

I reflected that as soon as we got the *Nijinsky* set up, we'd have to teach George and the kids intersystem code.

We? I thought suddenly. Funny . . .

The thought was fleeting, for suddenly sound burst

into the room. I could hear the humming of the machinery on the *Nijinsky* bridge, a lot of annoying mechanical sounds and static, and, almost pervasively the breathing sounds of the two kids.

Suddenly George came up.

"What in God's great heaven?" was all he could manage.

"Quiet!" I whispered. "Experiment!"

He stood there, and I started.

"Bridge to Gardeners 41 and 42," I called through the radio. It was horrible—my voice echoed and bounced all around and reflected back into the speaker. It was so great a sonic explosion that my big, sensitive ears barely caught, "Gardeners 41 and 42 standing by for instructions."

I smiled. Contact! It'd be hell, though. I wondered about their capabilities, but, I told myself, first things first.

"The insects are not insects at all," I told them, wishing I could hold my ears when I spoke, or shut them off a bit. I turned to George, finally moving over into the *Nijinsky* for a while, and he was wincing. I wished I could join him, and fleetingly hoped poor Marsha was either sound asleep or hadn't developed any of our hearing, yet.

"Not insects?" came the tinny reply. "But this ship is sterile. They are not-human. Therefore, they must be infestations."

"Not infestations!" I told them sharply. "They are humans."

"They are not-human," the machines persisted.

"Different kind of human," I told them, my head pounding from the sonic beating I was taking.

"We are programmed for but one kind of human," came the reply.

"This is a different kind of human," I argued. "You must accept them into your programming. The old humans are no more. These are the new-humans, the only humans."

There was silence, and I could almost hear their quasibiological relays considering and mulling over this statement. I could sympathize; they'd had a simple program, based on simple assumptions. Now they were being told that those assumptions were wrong, that their humans were not human but these new, strange, things were. It was impossible, inconceivable—and yet this information came from the bridge, to whom they were ultimately responsible. Here they had a contradiction. They would either accept it or they would switch off.

They accepted it.

"Not-human is human," they responded finally. "We acknowledge this new programming."

"You will accept voice programming and instructions only from the new-humans," I instructed. "Acknowledge."

"We acknowledge," came the reply.

"The new-humans speak in high frequencies," I told them. "Do you have the capability to receive them? What is your transducer frequency range?"

"We may receive any band selected up to one hundred thousand cycles," they replied.

I relaxed. Okay, then, we would be able to talk to them, although definitely *not* over voice radio. I wondered if they were advanced enough to learn intersystem code. I hoped so.

"I shall come to you now," I told them. "I will speak to you. You will adjust to my frequency."

"We understand," they replied. "Standing by."

"Eve!" I called. "Switch that thing off! Ham! Turn it down, then come back here!"

I broke contact, and almost collapsed, my ears ringing, my whole head feeling scrambled. I don't know how I managed to get through that ordeal, and I am very sure that I could never go through it again.

I lay there, collapsed in something of a heap, gasping for breath.

George came back in. "You're hurt," he said, noticing my wounds for the first time.

"I'm at the stage where I wish I would die and I'm afraid I will," I admitted. Even his voice beat like anvils in my head.

I heard Ham and Eve running down the corridor, and George turned to greet them.

"The kids will tell me what all this is about," he said gently. "I'll do whatever has to be done. You go below and collapse. We need you too much."

I started to protest, but I could barely get up, and they had to help me down the ramp.

"You smell like warmed-over piss," George said, a touch of revulsion in his tone. "After we get back I'll wash you off as best I can. Lay down near the shower."

I nodded, made it to the shower door, and collapsed knowing I could do nothing further except groan.

We didn't fit in the shower, of course, and it's ultrabeaming wouldn't stretch, but the basin was just outside and we used it as long as the water lasted.

George checked me over, and we went up first to hear the story of the robots from the kids and then to meet them. I hoped fervently that I'd been a hundred percent successful.

I ached so much I couldn't drop off, and I moved my head to look at Marsha.

In the short time I'd been gone, she'd changed. She lay there, stretched out on the grass, face up in a coma. She still wore the light jumpsuit, but I could see that it was already bulging a bit, stretching in odd places, and her head seemed slightly wider, a bit stretched. Her close-cropped hair was falling out; there were bald spots.

I lay, looking at her, and lapsed into unconsciousness.

There was a lot of noise, and people talking, when I awoke with a start.

I looked first at Marsha, who was out again on the grass. She was now greatly changed. Forelegs were well developed, the ears were well along, hind legs almost completely in. Her body was quite thin but properly proportioned for a Choz, and there was an even growth of body hair.

And she showed green.

Quickly noting this new development, I looked over at the bio lab console. It was an amazing sight.

George was there, and Eve, and they were running samples. I knew some of the stuff—all but the deeply analytical—could be done without me; but only through the computer could I translate and amplify the slides into sonic images George could understand.

George didn't need that anymore.

A huge, spiderlike shape was also there suspended upside down on the curved ceiling, and it was talking.

"The red area of number twenty-seven, chain three, is now throwing a pseudopod at eight degrees, holding color steady at blue-white," said an electronic voice.

George nodded to himself, apparently satisfied.

"Then it's time we started playing some tunes," he said lightly.

I jumped up. "What the hell?" was all I could manage.

George barely glanced at me. "Oh, hello, Bar. I was wondering if you'd ever wake up. Better eat something—we've been through two cycles since you conked out. How do you feel?"

"All right," I managed, still confused. I glanced up at the robot, memories of it or one like it in a similar pose much less pleasant in my mind. Seeing it again made me nervous.

"What's that thing doing here?" I asked suspiciously.

"It's helping us track the virus in her blood," Eve put in. "It can see in the same way the humans see."

Sure it could, I knew. "But—it's a gardener!"

155

"No, it's a utility robot programmed as a gardener," George responded. "Cheaper to make a standard model. You should know that. I'd assumed these things were a part of your everyday world."

I shook my head. "No, not ones looking like that. Wheeled ones, tracked ones, even roughly humanoid ones, but no spiders."

"Terraform unit model, obviously," the biologist decided. "And you have some deep-seated phobia against spiders."

It was true that I didn't like them very much, but I let the remark pass and started to eat to get my strength back.

"Any progress?" I asked between tubers.

"We're getting there," he replied.

"Getting there nothing!" Eve exclaimed admiringly. "He's practically got it, Bar! He's got samples from her blood doing tricks for him!"

I stopped and stared at the biologist. "That true?"

"Not exactly," he responded cautiously. "What I needed, what I couldn't really get from you, was a precise description of the molecular structure of the virus in the early stages. I've been handicapped by not having a sample of the original intestinal virus that Moses worked on—that's twenty years vanished in my memory. But it wasn't that complicated a thing, that I remember. I operated under the assumption that Moses' changes would be obvious mathematical alterations in the basic structure rather than a complete mutation. Remember, it's only been about fifty— sorry, fifty for me, about three hundred for you— years since we had electron microscopes capable of seeing something this tiny to begin with."

"And you've figured out what he did?" I prompted. You had to do this when George lectured, and everything on his subject quickly became a lecture. It was an adventure to him to be back in his profession after twenty years.

He nodded. "Oh, yes. That German fellow, Wenzel, solved some of the great mysteries of man, like what caused the common cold and about ninety types of cancer and various minor diseases. He also opened up some real problems—a whole new molecular biology. Here were creatures only thirty or so times the size of a hydrogen atom, yet with all the elements of life. There were lots of them, of course. I doubt if anybody's counted all the little critters yet. They're a new kind of life, a third kind, neither plant nor animal. We call them viruses only because that is what they most closely resemble."

"And you have the virus doing tricks?" I prodded again, insistently.

He shook his head, radiating mild derision. "Hardly," he said. "Oh, I've got it to stop growing when I tell it and speed up when I tell it, but that's all."

I looked at Eve and she gave me a see-what-I mean kind of expression.

"Do you mean to tell me," I said evenly, "that you have broken the code?"

"Oh, that much was simple," George replied with infuriating modesty. "Moses had a broad-beam broadcast signal that operated only in certain frequency ranges. Your experience with our robot friend, here, gave me the idea. If Moses controlled what the virus did, it had to do it by broadcast. We knew that much to begin with. And, to produce the stimulus-response mechanism, the colors, it had to result in our responding to a frequency to which the viruses also responded. Which? Well, obviously, it had to be at or close to the range of our own vision signals, somewhere between eighty thousand and a hundred and forty thousand cycles per second. Find that, do the minus sum of our vision, and you get Moses' frequency."

He made the whole thing sound so simple, and it wasn't. The logic steps involved were fantastic. It's

157

possible that nobody else would have been able to do it, and I said as much to George.

"Oh, no," he responded. "Probably half the colony could have—the Firsts, that is. When you expect to build a colony in an alien wilderness you need biology more than anything else."

"Well, maybe you're right," I told him, "but *I* wouldn't have figured it out, or even known what to look for. For the millionth time, I'm glad you're along for the ride, George."

He smiled, muttered something about the Lord working in mysterious ways, and returned to his work. I returned to eating, which took a little time.

Finally, I asked, "Where's Ham?"

"Up with Abel inventorying the cargo," George muttered, not looking up. "Abel can read, you know."

"Abel?" I asked.

"The other robot," Eve explained. "George named this one Cain and the other Abel."

I muttered something, but it was, thank heavens, unintelligible. George kept coming up with these zingers.

I decided I was better off elsewhere and returned to the *Nijinsky*.

It took some time to find Ham and—er, Abel. Ham greeted me enthusiastically, with the usual questions on how I was feeling and the like, then turned excitedly to the robot.

"He's been reading the mana-fistos or something big like that," he told me. "I don't know what he does, but he just looks at some place and instantly knows what's there. How's he do that, Bar?"

Memo to me, I thought seriously. Figure out a way for the Choz to have some kind of reading and writing. With the kind of families we had we couldn't depend on oral tradition.

"Well," I began, trying to explain. "It's something he can see and we can't. It's how the other robot can help George. Never mind about that now—what's on the ship?" God! It was tough and complicated being the founder of an alien race!

"We are mostly through, sir," the robot responded. "So far, skipping the smaller and personal items which we can itemize later, of the ten main holds we have in *A* five hundred thousand six hundred twenty-eight frozen food modules . . ."

Skip that. We'll toss it when we can, I thought.

". . . In *B*," Abel continued, "one million liters of distilled water . . ."

And did we ever need that! It would be our most precious commodity, I knew.

". . . In *C*, twenty-five construction robots, deactivated, types as follows . . ."

"Skip it," I told the robot. "Go on to the next."

"Very well," Abel responded, and I could swear I heard some sort of disdainful tone in his electronic speech, "in *D* the elements for a prefabricated modular village for eight hundred . . ."

Skip that, too, I thought, unless it had some extras in it we needed.

The one thing the Choz would never have is a housing shortage.

". . . In *E* construction lasers and boring tools," it continued, "in *F* a great deal of paraphernalia of unknown purpose and unstated on the manifest except as 'miscellany,' the same in *G* and *H*, *I* has chemicals and sealants of various types in containers, properly labeled as to each, and *J* has fifty kilometers of standard grass roll. The cargo bay, *K*, has, of course, the hothouse about which I believe you already know."

Did I ever, I thought sourly. But hold *J* excited me most of all—grass roll! If the virus took to it, and there was no reason to believe it wouldn't, we could carpet the whole *Nijinsky* in a Choz environment with lots of extras for later.

On reflection, the cargo wasn't especially unusual— exactly the sort of stuff one would send to a planet being Terraformed. The fact that so much of the stuff was useful to us was balanced by the amount that wasn't; how I would have loved to have gotten into one of the really big babies! I could almost taste it. Even with half the cargo gone, those behemoths would have more of the same and a lot to spare.

I was, on the whole, more than satisfied, though.

Baby Seiglein, I thought acidly, one of these days the ghosts of those you killed are going to rise up and haunt you good.

Sixteen

There was a lot of work to be done, a huge amount even for four Choz and two robots, mostly because the four Choz could do so little. We *could* get Cain and Abel to rig up sledges and tie tow ropes around us, though, and that simplified moving things around.

Do you know how long it takes to dispose of over half a million frozen dinners down a waste chute that was naturally, half a kilometer from the hold? Of course, I didn't let George do a lot. I wanted him to stay on the virus thing, so I borrowed Cain as I needed him to tie and rig stuff.

Things progressed in Choziforming the *Nijinsky*.

Marsha, too, progressed. I was there when she woke up, one stage from completion, a fully formed female Choz now but still without the horns with the vibrating membranes that would bring her sight of a new kind.

She struggled around, thrashing and disoriented.

"Hold it!" I warned. "Best to stay put for one more cycle. Then if you break your neck you'll at least see what you're doing!"

She looked around with the bemusement of the blind. "Who is that?" she asked.

"Bar Holliday, himself, his real voice," I responded lightly. "You're most of the way there."

She looked a little upset.

"Am I—do I look like you, now?" she asked hesitantly.

161

"Well, more like Eve—the green one." I told her. "You look fine to me."

She sighed and collapsed back on the grassy mat. "Was it like this for you?" she asked dejectedly. "I mean—was it this hard on you?"

"Of course," I replied sympathetically. "Hard on anybody not born to it, particularly when you don't have a choice in the matter. And me—I didn't even know what was happening to me. Neither did George."

She shook her head. "I don't believe it. You're too much in control of yourself. I know what scouts are like. I had two in my commune. Not that we saw them often—but they were just like you. Rock-steady, machines, able to cope with anything. That's the only reason I believed you—that manner, a way of talking that came through even the computer. That symbiosis with the ship. I knew you were telling the truth because you're that kind."

"Bullshit," I responded. "About that machinelike quality and total self-control. The others will tell you about how much of that I've had. It's a myth we create."

She shook her head sadly, then brought it up suddenly, listening.

"George isn't here?" she asked.

"No, he's over in the *Nijinsky* helping cut and position grass rolls," I replied. "There's nobody here but you and me."

"Then, listen," she said seriously. "I've talked a lot to George. I like him. He's more like me than like you. If it weren't for him I'd have asked you to throw me out with Nadya long ago. I actually *did* ask that once, but he talked me out of it."

I was surprised. It didn't fit my image of her. And this must have been fairly recently—she would have been able to hear him for only a cycle.

No of course not, I thought. There had been Cain, of course, to translate across the frequency gap.

"He told me about the bombing of this world," she said softly. "He told me about the place, its people, about how beautiful it was, how beautiful they were. About his daughter—Mara, wasn't it?"

I nodded, though she couldn't see it. "Eve's mother," I responded.

She sighed. "Yes. And with all that—here you are. George couldn't have done it, Bar, even if he'd known how to run this ship and could link with it. Seiglein would have fried him—fried almost anyone but a scout. Moses would have had anyone but a scout." She shifted a little, and I could feel her blind eyes staring at me.

"Do you remember how you felt when you discovered what had been done to that world?" she asked evenly.

"All the time," I responded sincerely. "The hurt is in me always."

"And you ranted and raved and kicked, I hear."

"I sure did," I admitted. "Some self-control!"

"George said he had wanted to kill himself and everyone else, but he knew you wouldn't let him."

I let that fall with a thud for a moment. George? Rock-solid George? The man who had calmed me down, cured my rage, reduced it to a dull ache?

Did I *ever* really consider what George was going through?

Suddenly I felt very, very small and very, very much like a rat. I said as much to Marsha.

"No! Don't!" she shot back. "Don't ever! You saved him, Bar Holliday! You saved him, and Ham, and Eve. He's a great man, Bar Holliday. So, in your own way, are you. It would have been even more tragic to have wasted that."

I was silent. I didn't agree with that last bit, but I couldn't think of anything to say.

"That's why I'm still here, still turning into this creature," she said after that long pause. "Talking to

George, watching you both, and the children—those incredible children, who sprang from you both. You're going to do something, the two of you. Something tremendous. I can feel it, even if I don't understand it. I want to be there, in the company of great men doing great things, Bar Holliday. If I cannot understand them, I can at least be a part of them. It is far greater than living a robotlike existence between commune and Creatovision on a milk run."

I smiled. I had been right after all about this woman, about the spark I'd seen in her at the start.

"Circumstances make great people and great events," I told her. "George was running from our world to some impossible utopia, and wound up a grass-eating plains animal. I flew to unknown places, it's true, but I flew for Seiglein, in the directions they told me, looking only for the things they wanted, pretending I was an independent big shot when all I really was after was gold stars to please the company. You're as much a part of that system as we. Believe it. We're all, equally, a pack of . . ." I searched for a word.

"Revolutionaries," came George's voice, and he hopped down the ramp. "That's what we are. Even changing our shape and form doesn't make us really different—inside, culturally—where it really counts. No, it's the real revolution we're after. That's why I'm so committed. Mankind's overdue for a revolution. The garden must be weeded or it'll die out of its own weight."

"But, George!" I objected. "We're not human anymore!"

He chuckled. "Physically we're the outward revolution Seiglein and the others fear, but they are a product of their own system. People have always judged others by form, by looks. People were hounded for their color, for their obesity, for slight defects from perfection. Well, we got rid of that. We bred ourselves into a race of ideal folk and we kidded ourselves that we were the best there was. No, the real revolutions are always from the inside, in the mind. *That's* the revolution, the one we really represent. So what if we turned everyone in the galaxy into Choz? How could you tell the difference, socially? Would people still have meaning in their lives? Bull. Patmos was an analog of human society. But not now, not anymore." He seemed to burn with a sudden fire. "We're going to bring them down."

Marsha turned to me. "See what I mean?"

I nodded, but I still didn't follow. George was certainly on his own track, one I didn't comprehend.

But George had been on the right track before.

Cycles came and went, and the work on the *Nijinsky* neared completion. The designers would never have recognized the place—nor, in fact, could Marsha.

She had a tough time getting the hang of being a Choz; she didn't have the advantage of being born to it, as did Ham and Eve, or of learning on open plains as George and I had.

Adjusting to Choz vision took several days, and it took much longer to use it unself-consciously. Movement took not only physical displacement but tremendous self-confidence, like the first time they put me in a ship, linked me to the computer, and said, "Fly it!"

Two out of three trainees, after years of prep, couldn't make themselves do it. Of those who could, only one in ten would develop enough confidence to try new things with a ship, to take it beyond orbital runs and see what it could do out in space, far from human aid. And of those, like Marsha, only one in thousands confident enough to become a part of their ships, become scouts like me.

It was a matter of pride, and yet it boiled down to self-confidence. The self-confidence that made you go out and come back. The self-confidence, perhaps the bull-headedness, to refuse to admit defeat.

Marsha had to fall a lot of times, hurt herself a lot of times, before she could get around unaided. She didn't enjoy being a Choz, but she accepted it. Accepted it and worked at it. I was proud of her.

"We were lucky, George," I said one day. "Lucky to get one like her at random."

"Naw," he scoffed. "They're there—probably millions of them. The ones still adaptable. They're dying out, being replaced by nonadaptable, unthinking Nadyas. But the ones with the spark—they need to be broken free, shown there's a better way. Back on old Earth there once reigned huge lizards, called dinosaurs. Enormous. Tons and tons. They couldn't adapt, and they died. Now it's our turn. Space has delayed it, and provided something of an outlet that has kept the creative, adaptive spark alive, if dormant. I'll bet there'll be a Marsha in every ship, or at least in every other ship! Those are the ones we're saving, boy! We're going to de-dinosaur them!"

He talked more and more this way as time passed, and I pursued the subject less and less with him. Instead I spent a great deal of time with Marsha, getting to know her well. We had a definite affinity of the kind impossible to explain—emotional, mental, maybe. Not the physical, certainly. That's not a Choz characteristic. We enjoyed each other, liked being with each other, talking things out. I had never really enjoyed this experience before, nor had she.

Ham and Eve were maturing fast, but they'd had George and me to themselves all their lives. They were jealous of this newcomer, and it took some time to break them down.

Although Eve was my daughter, she identified most closely with George and his interests. I think she fairly worshiped the man, and I knew it embarrassed him no end. She was becoming a proficient biotechnician in the process. George loved to teach, and Eve wasn't handicapped by George's previous training, with its dependence on hands and eyes.

It was Marsha herself who finally broke Ham's stubborn resistance to and withdrawal from our social communion. She taught him to operate the *Nijinsky*.

In the meantime, with the help of Cain and Abel, we had managed to prepare the habitat for what had to come, sooner and sooner now.

We'd cleared out all the cargo holds that held material useless to us and jettisoned the stuff. Pressurizing the holds and linking them to the general ship's biomonitoring systems, we lined them with grass roll and planted just a few of the tubers from our garden.

The virus took to the carpet like mad. In only a few cycles *our* grass was competing with the original grass, and we had large areas of new grazing land.

Arranging the grass roll and cutting it with the robots' help, we lined every place we could except the ramp wells and the bridge area. Within forty cycles, the *Nijinsky* was a floating, self-contained Choz biosphere. Choz grass contributed so much additional oxygen to the air we had to turn down the recycling system: We couldn't breathe it as fast as the plants could spit it out, so it was carbon dioxide, not oxygen, that we had to add.

As for George, with my help through the computer and with the eyes and tentacles of Cain and Abel, he had made great progress. "I think I can control the virus pretty well," he told me one day. "I can step it up, slow it down, or make it dormant. A slight modification and I can mildly mutate it so that it will have no effect on anything except Choz and Patmos material. It's simple, really—just took infinite patience in sorting out the code groups. It helped to have your computer—I described Moses' logic system, and that narrowed it down. I can even produce the secretion that breaks down things selectively, if I can be linked to the computer to get the analytical information the virus transmits on molecular composition."

"You can do everything Moses could, then," I responded, awed.

"Not quite." He shook his head slowly. "No, I don't have the original virus mutant he worked with. I doubt we could ever match the conditions existing in the original organism. And without it I can't alter the present pattern."

I frowned, puzzled. "So? What does that mean?"

"It means," he replied, "that I can do anything with the virus Moses programmed into it—and there are probably lots of things we don't even know about, which will need discovering before I can do them. But I can't change the basic pattern. I can make humans into Choz, but not Choz into humans. Same with the vegetables."

Marsha had been fascinated by the conversation, but when he said that last her tone changed to mild sadness and disappointment. "Then," she said, "we're Choz forever."

One day the inevitable happened. George called me over.

"What's the matter, George?" I called cheerfully. "You look too serious."

"Been noticing things lately?" he asked enigmatically.

I looked puzzled. "What do you mean?"

"I noticed Ham acting funny earlier, and asked him what the matter was. He didn't know, so I looked into it. We'll be acting funny soon ourselves, Bar. You haven't noticed it yet because you're in love with her and lovers always feel differently."

"Marsha?" I asked, more confused than ever.

He nodded. "She's a deeper green today, Bar. She'll get more and more that way. She doesn't know it, of course. That's not the system. And Eve—well, she's not likely to notice it, either."

I thought for a minute. "The Breed," I said at last. "She's coming into it."

He nodded. "She turned as an adult, remember,

like you. Eve's due not long from now, so we've got to remember that, too. If Ham reacts to Marsha, that means they're both physiologically about two now—adults."

"So?" I responded. "We've known about it. That's why we have the *Nijinsky*, and did all this work."

"There's three males and only two females," he said slowly. "Ever think of that?"

I hadn't, but I didn't see what difference it made.

"You've never been through one on the plains," he noted. "You never were driven crazy, battling all the males for whoever you got. It's bad news, and it can result in a lot of jealousy and bitterness. One of us has to lose, and it feels lousy to lose at the Breed."

"So what do we do?" I asked him. "After this, there won't be a problem."

He nodded. "Well, I can control things pretty well, you know. I can send the signals for almost anything. Since Moses was able to control the number of eggs in the last Patmos Breed, I can do it, too. With Eve's help, I've already done the preliminary work."

"Then you could also stop the Breed," I pointed out.

He nodded. "I could, but we need people. Badly. I want a manageable number, but a reasonably large one. There are five of us—we can raise two each, I think, handle ten as a co-op venture. I want more Hams and Eves, not the Patmos vegetables. We need the time to raise them right."

I agreed, and asked for his plan.

"Well, we'll arrange it for five each. To stop this stupid contest, I'm going to suppress my own sexual drives. I can manage that, with the computer's help and your link, I think."

"I think you should be one of the parents," I objected. "We need more of you. Ham can wait."

He shook his head. "No, I don't want him to. I think it's about time he had some responsibility. And

—well, you'll take Marsha, of course. Eve—well, she's *your* daughter, of course, but she—she reminds me a great deal of Mara."

"She *is* of Mara," I pointed out.

"Of course," he acknowledged. "But it's more than looks. It's manner, mind, curiosity. Personality, I guess. After all, I raised them both, in a way. Plenty of time for me. I'll sit this one out."

He instructed me on what to do, how to play certain tones pitched so high even we couldn't hear them, aimed at his genitals and at certain areas in his brain and body.

We called Marsha from the *Nijinsky*. For the first time I noticed what George was talking about. She was getting that bright-green glow that Mara had had when we left her village for the point. I felt a slight stirring within me that had probably been present all along, but of which I was only now conscious.

George nodded satisfactorily. "She looks normal to me," he said. "How about you?"

"You're right," I told him. "I can feel it now."

He smiled. "Good. I was afraid that the code tones might have zapped you, as well. Now, I'll handle Ham and Eve. I want you two to go into Hold A and lock yourself in until afterward. That way we won't have problems with Ham."

I nodded, and went over to Marsha.

"What's this all about?" she demanded. "You two are acting very conspiratorial."

And I told her. Oh, we'd told her before, academically, but the Breed was always some time in the future in our discussions, not to consider "now," particularly not to us. Like all spacers, myself included, she'd been sterilized when she entered flight school. Most people were sterilized anyway, of course, but with spacers that was mandatory. Can't risk birth defects or mutations.

At first she laughed and refused to believe it. "You

mean—you mean I'm actually going into heat, like an animal? Oh, wow! And you can *see* it?"

I nodded. "And Ham, too. That's why we've got to closet ourselves away."

But first we let George play supersonic music over her.

Two days later, in Hold A, Marsha discovered what it was like. As I said before, little thought was possible during the whole ritual; it was programmed, although pleasant. Even building the web-house together was part of it, although such a thing was hardly needed with us. It was still a fantastic, beautiful work of art, the first any of the entire five-person Choz race but George or I had ever seen. After the ten-day-long vigil, there were the eggs. Five of them, as George had ordained. Five this time, four for her extremely enlarged pouch, one for my normal one.

After the great sleep, we awoke, as from a coma, a pleasant, orgasmic coma, and she shook her head in wondrous disbelief.

George had explained the length of the ritual. The viral strains used in the process matched themselves to the two partners, and needed the time to build, to control, to form those eggs.

They replaced genes in the Choz biosystem, but they had to work harder for it.

Marsha's first words after it was over were: "That's incredible!"

I smiled. "Every two years, you know. More often for me later on."

She nodded. "It's a wonderful thing, really." She looked back at the glistening silver of the web-house. "You know, I was trying to imagine a place of trees and fields and cities of web-houses like this. I can't. But it's *so* beautiful—it must have been a wonderful place."

"It could have been," I responded gently. "Could have been—if it had existed without Moses' overbearing control and sense of mission. That is part of what we're working for now, here. Another Patmos, a place as wonderful as that dead world could have been, but with only ourselves in control."

She weaved her head slowly from side to side.

"It's funny. I can hardly feel them. The eggs, that is."

I nodded. "You won't for a while. George and I even forgot about ours. But they start growing, hatching, building, hanging kinda heavy on you after a bit— and you are carrying four times what I had. They don't let you forget in the end."

Later, when we'd rested and eaten to replenish our depleted bodies, we broke down the webbing that sealed the hatch and went over to the scout.

I had been most nervous about leaving George in charge. There was always the infinitely small risk of mechanical breakdown or discovery—and both pilots had been incapacitated for ten days.

If necessary Ham could have taken us into the jump, so we weren't totally defenseless.

George greeted us warmly, and the questions from Eve—and those tinged with a slight jealousy from Ham —were incessant. They were answered better less than ten cycles later, when we sealed them into Hold A for their first time.

In twenty more cycles Marsha produced, one at a time, first four heads and forelegs, then, when they dropped, Ada, April, Ann, and Aud.

Marsha decided to name them by the alphabet, as long as it lasted, to keep track of the generations. It was a good, rational system.

I, too, had a daughter, being the freak. I named her Mara.

Eve's four offspring George named in characteristic fashion, although, abandoning his monosyllabic tradition for once. Judith, Esther, Ruth, and Mary.

Ham had a son, which he allowed George to name Matthew.

The Web of the Chozen

We were a family and a race of fifteen now.

Time passed, and it was full. I used it to raise my share, and to develop the writing system I wanted. It wasn't very good at the start, and we used computer storage until we started to run out of it, but it worked and developed. Had I had some way to manufacture things, I could have done better, but we managed, with effort, to create a primitive sort of paper out of mashed vegetation, very fragile but it had to do. And, from that, a system of pinholes, painstakingly punched in prearranged patterns with an awl or some other sharp tool held in the mouth. But you could scan the holes, read what was written in the code, which I based on the intersystem code that every spacer was taught.

And I told my lies, my spacefaring lies, to new generations, and Marsha, who'd heard those stories too many times, topped them often with her own.

Time passed, as a small group became a tiny civilization. Each succeeding Breed was limited to two females and one male (except for mine, which George managed to get limited to two, period) so we kept our ratio, our family, our mission, and roughly two females per male. By careful manipulation, George managed our society and we stayed without the strife and breed contention we had feared.

And George never seemed to run out of names.

Occasionally we'd seal the *Nijinsky* and I'd take a run into the human sector to check on it, to intercept radio signals, and, once in a while, to raid a beacon for additional water. Since the *Nijinsky* hadn't moved, and used no fuel at idle, we needed little of it.

There was always the temptation to raid another freighter, but we'd been lucky once, and then they were Terraforming that world.

Time passed, and the living was pretty good.

In five breeds, we had 891 females and 445 males and the *Nijinsky* was full.

"We can't afford another Breed," George said to

me one day. "We're really over the limit now. There's some room, yes, but water is getting stretched very thin, and we can't recycle all of it."

I agreed. The time had been wonderful, but our odd race of space-born herbivores, only three of whom had ever seen planetfall, was at the do-or-die point. Nothing lasts forever.

We'd debated the point endlessly, George, Marsha, and I. The people were ready for a move—our own stories had fueled a desire for a place of their own in the universe. But deciding to act and deciding *how* to act are two different things.

Marsha, bless her, had a much shorter fuse than we.

"Look," she said, exasperated. "You, Bar, you want revenge on the corporations, on humanity, on Seiglein. I've heard it on and off, on and off, for too many years. You're stuck." She turned on George. "And you—you want some sort of moral crusade to break the system. Well, nobody's thought of me—me and the rest of our people. We want a home, that's all. A home. And to hell with revenge and moral crusades! You two haven't stopped being little boys since you dragged me into this! Well, it's about time you grew up! You're responsible for all of us—you have to do not what you want but what is best for us!"

When she got started, she cut with a nasty knife. She was the real political organizer of the colony, anyway; the closest thing to a matriarch or an ancient queen I'd ever experienced.

"Oh, shit, Marsha," I moaned when she was through. "What's your idea, anyway?"

She smiled. "You remember all those old Creatovision plots we had as kids?" She nodded to George. "He doesn't—that was before him. But you know where I'm going. I think it's almost time we did the old alien plot for real."

I chuckled, liking what she had in mind the more I thought of it. Of course George knew the plot—it was probably as old as man's awareness of other planets, but I had to explain it.

"She means," I said, barely restraining my mirth at the mental images the idea was already conjuring up, "that the alien monsters from outer space should invade a planet."

Seventeen

Back when I was very small, and Seiglein's Total Care Center #31 was my whole world, the only escape from routine was Creatovision. Oh, not the superfancy type, with the programmable plots, but there you were, with a couple of friends, in somebody else's body (as far as you were concerned), going through tremendous adventures. Sea stories could make you seasick, and if you hated the smell of salt-spray or feared the depths they were not for you. Westerns could give you very real psychosomatically induced saddle sores; love stories of the period we generally avoided.

But the kind of program that used to get to you, *really* get to a young child, was the invasion plot. There were lots of invasion plots—endless variations on it, just as there were endless variations of the other plots, but this was a special one.

It was designed to scare the hell out of you.

The monsters, usually from some kind of weird civilization, would arrive secretly by spaceship and creep up on unsuspecting towns on newly Terraformed worlds—always new ones. I guess it's a lot harder to be convincing if you're invading a superquad of three thousand prefabs. Usually the monsters would take over your best friend, or all your neighbors, and they'd march around looking weird and giving ultimatums to the government to give in or they'd take over all the civilized worlds.

Some superscientific genius, usually with the Huang

Corporation logo, would always arise, and figure out the indivisible zap ray that would drive them out of the captive bodies.

Afterward we'd huddle together in the dorms and talk nervously about our own experiences, seeing aliens in every dark corner, sleeping with the lights on, looking strangely at Comrade Juni who's been acting funny lately.

Now, here we were in the scout (no use risking the *Nijinsky* or the rest of the colony), Marsha, George, a dozen or so others, and me, sitting off a world cast adrift but still in the process of being Terraformed, maybe fifty years from superquads and prefabs, considering how to go about taking over this place called St. Cyril by the charts.

We were fifteen weird, nonhuman creatures, all but three spawned in a strange and unnatural environment, looking for a planet to take over, running through the plans one last time, checking the wording on our ultimatum. The alien invaders at last were poised to strike, as all of us kids knew they would someday, the evil mastermind directing it from his spaceship too advanced and fast to be caught.

And here I was—me, the evil mastermind, directing the scenario.

It pained me that I would not actually be a party to the raid; I was too valuable to lose—the only man who could direct the scoutship. But with George's creative help, we would be able to hear, in some cases even see, what was going on, much as Moses had done back on Patmos.

Marsha was going, though, as the on-site leader. She knew more about the layouts of colony worlds, what funny shapes would be what, than anyone else.

I was nervous, not just for the mission, but for her. This planet wasn't particularly far along as yet; there could be all sorts of hidden dangers out there, perhaps even weapons.

Our communications system was a marvel. In some

ways, it was much like telepathy, although the basis was bionic. George could receive selectively sound waves returning from any of the party as the modulated information on a radio frequency carrier. After subtracting the carrier wave the resulting sound patterns within the common Choz frequency range could be interpreted as pictures or sound—as if we were sending and receiving the sonar or talking ourselves. It was an eerie feeling—I'd participated in many of the tests. Like being in somebody else's body, yet totally without control of it.

Those of us on the ships could send, too—although only in a common frequency band. That, also, took some getting used to, since everyone in the landing party would receive anything we said. It was agreed that, unless something extraordinary came up, all communications would be addressed to Marsha, whom we would monitor as the standard—again, unless there was a reason to switch.

The auras of the landing party showed them to be excited, expectant—and nervous as hell. Marsha was even more scared than the others, a good sign, I felt. A scared leader is a cautious one.

All we really needed to do to accomplish our purposes was to land and take off, but this wasn't a ship, it was a *planet*. First, the virus might not take to it—there might be some sort of radiation or something mutated in the vegetation that would stop it. Then, of course, there was size—though it was a small planet, it was huge by any other standard. Moses began on Patmos with four tiny areas; we didn't know how long it had taken him to Choziform the savannas in their entirety, but George guessed it must have been years. Perhaps that affected the timing of the reproductive cycle. Who knew how Moses thought?

We couldn't wait. We wanted only a small patch at the start, and yet it had to demonstrate the ongoing process.

We had to be *seen*.

I took one last survey of the place. A great deal of heat radiation from several areas, a smaller amount from a third to the north. The probe said it was warm enough for the virus, although colder than it liked for optimum performance.

The radiation survey did indicate a minor settlement, possibly a construction camp. I could get no more from my instruments, built for eyes, so that would have to be that.

I called out, "Ready!" and went in fast, braking at the last possible moment, putting them about two kilometers from the site of the radiation. The automatic pressure equalization system was activated, and, when that was done, I opened the air-lock door. The scoutship, shaped much like a spade in a card deck, rested on a bed of fifty-centimeter springlike supports all over its underside, which kept me level.

A chill wind blew in through the hatch; I turned to Cain, perched so he could see the direct readout instruments.

"Temperature?" I asked.

"Sixteen degrees Celsius," he responded.

"Humidity?"

"Seventy-one point six percent," the robot read.

I turned to the raiding party, an auspicious thirteen in number.

"Take care," I said softly to Marsha, but she didn't reply. I started the takeoff sequence setup. . . .

"Go!" I yelled, and, like that, they were out, out into the night of the funny little woodland world.

As soon as they were clear I closed the lock, activated the autosterilization procedures, and hit the throttle hard. We jerked, but it wasn't nearly as bad as the L-jump despite the sustained pressure of a fast takeoff.

George and I were alone in the ship.

"I'm parking, George," I told him. "We're in stationary orbit over them now. You can plug in any time."

George nodded. He was actually plugging in two different things; we would share the experiences, since the data came to the computer, then had to be channeled to the open panel through me.

But George held the keys to the keyboard.

We faced the jury-rigged transceiver panel, built with the computer's knowledge of circuitry and the tentacles of Cain and Abel from parts taken from the *Nijinsky*.

The panel was showing pictures. Sound pictures, as the Choz saw.

"It's working," I breathed. George was silent, expectant, tense.

Marsha looked around. Lots of tall trees, most rising thirty meters or more before they had any sort of branches or leaves. Thick groves of them, covering the sky, shutting out sunlight. The ground was bare except for some very primitive, mosslike growths.

She checked the nine males and three females chosen for the party. Each had specialized training or the personality for this sort of thing in our opinion— but who could know? Who could anticipate everything and everyone?

That hesitant thought went through Marsha's mind, but she knew it was too late to have reservations.

"This way, quickly and silently," she ordered, then started off through the growth. They followed, quickly adjusting to the slightly less than normal gravity that gave them for the first time in their lives the freedom to truly leap, to almost fly. As they moved there were sounds all around them, the most pervasive seemed like a huge singing group, humming. It was a constant tone, although it rose and fell in pitch as they passed one spot or another.

Some sort of insect, Marsha guessed, and kept on.

She almost stopped, causing a minor collision, when something small and yellow scurried across the little clearing in front of her, but she kept hold of herself and just continued loping on, knowing that this was yet something of a wild world, one with little things that hummed and others that scurried.

Within minutes, they broke through the edge of the forest.

They were on the edge of an escarpment, rather gentle but long; a plain, with Terran-style groves and even a sprinkler system of sorts covering most of it; at the base and off a few hundred more meters was the camp—a town, really, with electricity that radiated as dull red heat to her eyes, and a single, familiar four-pattern of prefabs.

They took some time to survey the scene, to get to know it. The night sky was no help, but the lights were enough illumination for the basics of the color sense, as was the brightness that was a close, rocky neighbor planet of roughly equal size, reflecting the sun.

"The humans are in the buildings, there," she told them, voice set and determined. "The large block to the right, there, houses the construction and maintenance robots. It's entirely possible that we might meet a utility robot or two in the groves. If so, avoid it if possible. Your fear index will trip the disabling tone if things get too bad, and we will be there to help."

They crept down through groves of some sort of vegetable, occasionally getting wetted down by the sprinklers, but they met no human or robot as they progressed.

Almost at the village, they came to a sudden clearing and Marsha's hooves clattered against something hard. She looked down, sounding it, but it took a few seconds to realize what it was.

"A road!" she exclaimed. "A service road! Bar! Can you trace the road? Does it go a good distance? Is there a landing place well down it?"

I ordered the photo probe from ship's sensors, but the pictorial was a blank to me.

"Cain?" I shot to the robot. "You heard?"

"The road does not go far," responded the robot. "It runs into a network of other smaller roads, and one very large one going off to the southwest."

"The longest one will do," I responded. "Is there a landing place two or more kilometers from any settled area?"

"There is," the robot replied. "I shall feed you its coordinates."

He did and I stored the information in the computer. I turned back to Marsha and her group.

"What you got in mind, hon?" I asked her.

"Roads mean cars and trucks of some kind," she pointed out. "That means water tanks for the irrigation system. We might as well get something out of this other than moral satisfaction."

I thought it over, looked at George. He shrugged. "Will it fit in the lock?" he asked.

"Depends," I responded. "Hon, if you can find one that fits, go to it. Anything else, too. Otherwise, raise your hell and git."

She nodded, then suddenly froze.

There was the sound of a whirring motor somewhere near, approaching.

"Quickly!" she called to the others. "Into the bushes and freeze!"

They didn't need any extra urging. She took a mighty leap and was so far back she risked edging forward to get a view of the road.

There was a truck coming, a little angular affair, with single headlight. A three-wheeler. She scanned to see the driver, but there was no driver. It was an automated vehicle.

Nobody moved, nobody breathed, as the thing came up to within a few meters of them, whirred past, and vanished down the road without a pause.

"Whew!" she breathed. "Nervewracking, that. Well, c'mon, gang. Let's head into town."

They proceeded slowly to the edge of the quad. Many lights were on, she could tell by the colors reflecting off the grassy center plot, but there seemed to be no one stirring outside.

"Damn!" she exclaimed angrily. "No trucks. Well, okay, then." She turned to the group. "Anybody feel like they have to shit?"

Several did, in fact, and she urged them to do it in the quad, on the grass, depositing as they did huge cultures of the virus.

The operation needed a little more light, but you could almost swear that the edges of the grass around the three piles of manure were turning a dull pink even now.

"Look at the piles!" George cut in sharply. "Keep looking until I tell you to stop!"

They complied, and he played little tunes to the piles relayed by the Choz to the ground. He was instructing the virus as to its rate of multiplication, I knew, stepping everything up to maximum speed.

Near the end of this, someone decided to come out of one of the quads.

We heard the door slide open, and switched to the first Choz who looked up. Someone—looked like a man, hard to tell with the baggy clothes. He was humming something, and he started across the area, hardly looking where he was going.

"Everybody!" I called. "Contact!"

He almost bumped into Marsha.

"Excuse me," he mumbled, face still staring at the ground.

He saw something strange there, and his face came up, meeting Marsha's gaze.

His mouth opened, and he screamed so terribly we could feel it way up in orbit. The man was terrified.

He started to back away, then just stood, a few meters back, gaping. Marsha lost her patience, and made a feint for him, and he screamed again and ran as fast as he could back to the door from which he'd emerged, yelling and screaming.

There were the sounds of movement, calls, and some additional lighting snapped on, making the quad a blaze of color.

"Scatter!" she yelled at them. "Meet back at the road when you're done!"

They leaped in all directions. One headed for the generating plant off to one side, another to the water system, yet others to their assigned stations. Marsha stood her ground and glared at the lights she could sense but not see.

"Okay, you bastards! C'mon out and fight!" she yelled, although they could not hear her.

Three humans acted as if they did, though. There was no way of telling if one was our first contact—they tended to look alike to us, I discovered—but they came out of the same building and gaped at her for a moment.

She turned and faced them, scanning them carefully. One held what seemed to be a wrench. No other weapons were visible. The one with the tool appeared to be the leader, and he advanced on her, the others following cautiously, nervously.

"Hey, beastie," he whispered gently. "Nice beastie. What are ye, beastie? C'mon to Papa Njumo now, take it easy. . . ."

He kept murmuring reassuringly, but the wrench was held in a nasty way.

Marsha let him approach, doing a wide scan to make certain there were no surprises. There were several other humans in open doorways, but these three were the only ones that made any kind of move.

"Jeez! What the hell *is* it?" one of the nervous followers managed. "I ain't never seen nothin' like it before. Them *eyes*—jeez!"

"Shut up!" Njumo ordered sharply through clenched teeth and broad smile. "If I can get close in enough I can brain it, I think." His tone softened again. "Nice beastie, come to Papa, beastie . . ."

"Why, that son of a bitch!" Marsha exploded, and leaped high into the air at the trio. She judged her distance perfectly as only a Choz can gauge a leap, forehooves pushing the two men behind Njumo, hind legs kicking into Njumo's shoulders and, perhaps, his skull as she gave an extra push in the air for effort.

She crashed into the two men, and sprawled with them. Choz aren't light—she weighed a hundred fifty kilos if she weighed one—and when she rolled over onto one of them he screamed in pain. She recovered quickly as the buildings erupted with construction personnel, mostly yelling conflicting orders and running around, watching her warily.

Scanning that the three she tackled were out for the count, she whirled and poised for another spring.

"Watch it!" I warned anxiously. "They can hurt you, you know!"

"The hell with them!" she sneered. "God! It's been so long! They're so small, so soft, so slow! Hah! I'll show 'em what a Choz woman can do!"

She leaped at a bunch, who were taken aback both at the speed and the duration of the leap—perhaps twenty, twenty-five meters!

I knew what she was feeling, feeling for the first time—the power of the Choz in the open, the freedom, the tremendous control when we were in a place like that for which we were designed.

She hit a row of men and women who froze in fear as she came upon them, like some flying horror. She struck the first two, and they careened into others. It was almost comical the way they fell into each other, going down in sequence.

"Get one of the borers from the construction shed!" someone yelled. "Nail it!"

She spotted the woman who yelled it, probably a construction foreman, and leaped again, tearing into her.

"Marsha!" I yelled. "Get the hell out of there! Enough, already!"

She was breathing hard, but it was more from excitement than the exercise.

"Hell, no!" she responded. "Let's *really* give them something to remember!"

With that, she leaped for an open doorway, and entered the building. She knew her way well enough, as would I; they were all alike, every one, everywhere.

There were no locks in the perfect society; she bounded up the short stairs and nudged the panel next to a second-floor apartment. The door slid open, barely large enough for her, and she barged in.

A woman was in there, totally nude, watching the excitement from her window. She turned as Marsha stormed in, and screamed. Marsha stopped, then slowly approached the terrified woman. She shied back into a corner, trapped. Marsha approached her, so close that the woman could smell her breath.

Then the power-drunk Choz smiled—I don't know how I know that, but I do—and caressed the woman in some nasty places with her tongue. Her fun over, she shot some webbing at those nasty places and turned for the window.

The quad was full of people; she could hear them, but the window blocked the sonar. They were the sealed type, too. No way.

"Marsha!" I screamed. "No!"

She charged the window, striking it first with her huge, extremely powerful hind feet, smashing the plasticine into millions of tiny crystals. Still almost ten meters up, she straightened out, and had the sounding before she landed.

"If I hadn't seen it with my own eyes I wouldn't have believed it," George murmured.

The quad was a sea of humans now, but there were other things there as well.

"Marsha!" I yelled. "Robots! Get out of there! Jump over if you can!"

They were the big kind, the construction kind, not easily bypassed. They had the quad hemmed in, and the humans quickly retreated behind them, leaving her exposed.

She stood her ground, but she was scared again now, suddenly, in the face of those huge, terrible machines.

"They've got me cut off!" she almost yelled in panic. "I don't—"

"Why doesn't the protective sound come?" I shouted at George.

George was transfixed. "I don't—unless . . . Oh, my God! You remember all the times we saw it, right from the start! It was always the males, Bar! Always the males! Never Eve, never the others!"

He was right, I knew with certainty. In that Bible that Moses and George followed in different ways, women were the weaker, dependent sex.

"Everyone! All males! Get to that quad! Marsha needs you!" I yelled.

"Ahead of you!" came several responses, but a quick check showed they were a short distance away.

"George!" I called. "Do you have enough virus to disable them?"

He shook his head. "One, maybe. No more!"

Not in many years had I felt so helpless, so cheated. Nobody, I thought angrily, beats Bar Holliday.

My head cleared. "George! Get that virus to the operators! The robots can't shoot any animal life on their own!"

The great things were closing in fast. They wanted a narrow field of fire, to avoid hitting the buildings.

"Locked in!" George called. "Marsha! Scan the cabs!"

She had panicked and was looking every which way, but she snapped out of it.

George played some tones, first at one, then the second, then the third. The fourth, however, he missed, and the first three weren't instant; it would take time for the virus to start dissolving their clothes, causing the diversion.

Then suddenly, four more were there, behind them, and we saw the clouded vision of the panic defense in action. Things seemed to slow—but George jumped.

"The laser!" he yelled. "One of them is on and we can't see it!"

Marsha looked confused, then sprang in a giant leap right at one of the lumbering automatons.

A beam followed, we found, slicing off a section of the construction robot she'd landed alongside.

The operator of that one was frozen by the defense sounds, feeling too much pain to react, and she was able to jump again.

The wild laser lashed through, out of control, and beyond the two other robot borers. Pieces of machinery were chipped off, and flew, and the beam cleared, striking out. We saw Marsha's vision blur as something hit her. She screamed and dropped like a stone.

"The hell with this!" I growled. "I'm going in!"

We dropped suddenly down almost to the edge of town. I opened the lock anxiously and called the others.

"Marsha's hurt!" came a call from one of the others, I couldn't tell which. "And so's Shem! Bring litters!"

We had a couple for emergency purposes, and Cain strung one quickly around me.

"Stay here, George!" I commanded as the older man made to follow. "Cain! Come with me!"

The robot scuttled out the lock, and I kept up as best I could, dragging the sledge.

It wasn't far to the site. I didn't have time for recriminations—the males couldn't hold that panic beam deliberately, and I knew it might quit at any time, bringing the laser canons to bear on us.

Cain picked up two limp forms and put them on the sledge; one of the women spun webbing to hold them, and I was off, Cain pacing me.

I made the lock and dropped the web-rope from my teeth.

"George! Get them back here!" I ordered crisply. "Let's go!"

I started the emergency takeoff procedures, and counted anxiously as first one, then all the others fairly leapt into the air lock. I closed it, fed the pressurization in, and gunned it. Ship's sensors showed two bulky shapes closing fast, and I knew that I would have little time to spare.

We were far out into space when I dared relax, having made the short L-jump as quickly as I could match vector and velocity.

Only then I was able to look at the two injured Choz.

One, a male caught in the wild fire, was obviously dead—perhaps the first Choz of the new breed to die. A Fourth, Shem had been a good, inquisitive boy with a knack for mechanical concepts, I remembered sadly.

Marsha was still alive, although that was almost a matter of opinion. She was out cold, and I surveyed the damage. A part of her left ear gone, some teeth broken, and—

Her hind legs were gone, as if sliced off by a giant meat cleaver, along with her tail. There was massive hemorrhaging, but George was at work with his tone board and seemed to be winning that battle, a battle that needed to be won quickly.

"She needs a transfusion," George said after a while. "No, don't jump to volunteer. We haven't anything to do it with. I've done the best I can for now, and we'll just have to wait. If she makes it—well, then we'll see."

I bit my lower lip in anxiety. "George," I said gravely. "Suppose—suppose she does pull through, somehow. Can the virus—regenerate that much?"

He shook his head. "I have no idea. If anybody can pull through, she will. She's got guts, that girl—

and one hell of a bullheaded will to live. As for regeneration—I don't know. In a stable Choz—well, this sort of thing's never happened on this scale before."

I was terrified. I didn't know what I'd do without Marsha to keep me in control, to provide my common sense. In a way, she was like a part of me—for so long a time now. I looked mournfully at the old man.

"George—what—what am I going to do?" I asked, voice breaking.

He looked straight at me. "Go ahead with the plan, of course. There's 1,332 other Choz to think of, you know."

Eighteen

Several hours later we broke jump near the beacon we had selected earlier. By now, we knew, St. Cyril would have frantically radioed for help, and the government and the Nine Corporations, Seiglein included, would know what had gone on. Seiglein, at least, would also know from the description of the weird creatures just what the implications were—and just who was behind it.

The ghost of Patmos had struck at last.

Seiglein would know, too, from the descriptions of the strange new stuff growing not only in the quad patch but in other places we'd been, just what was going to happen. He'd know that, when the stuff spread, it would cover the whole patch around the camp, then start hitting the men and women in the camp when the food supply warranted, changing them, transforming them into Choz in that four-day ritual.

Adult Choz would breed as the virus itself spread, and spread it still more, over the face of the whole temperate zone of the planet.

Soon—maybe a year, maybe two, no more—the virus, carried on air currents through the wind patterns of the world, would hit one or both of the cities established as prototypes on St. Cyril, the larger areas of heat radiation we'd detected.

How many? Thousands would undergo the Change, and survivors, sane and insane, would undergo the Breed as well. Victims of our invasion. Victims soon incapable of using the tools to help them, cut off from humankind by its very real understanding that any contact with the virus could prove disastrous.

Ship's sensors scanned the area as clean, and I linked with the beacon, equalized, and went aboard. It had been ten years or more since I'd been in one of these at all—the last time, too, as a Choz—asking help.

Now, as I manipulated the controls, set up the computer link, and sent one of the males, Jon, to be my visual stand-in, I was in a different position, one of power, one of command.

If only Marsha weren't lying there, trying to hold on to a slender life thread, all of it would have been perfect.

"To Seiglein," I began my transmission recording. "This is Bar Holliday. You remember me. Once I worked for you; then, when it was most needed, I appealed to you for help—and got genocide and my own attempted murder. Well, things are different now, Seiglein. I have just hit, as you must know, the new colony of St. Cyril. I have started irreversible changes of a nature you know well. That was a sample."

I paused for effect, then continued. "You can see what it is doing to St. Cyril. Think what it would do to Derwin, or Yinching or even Earth. You can't defend against it, you can't fight it. I can pick any of the hundred and three plus worlds, any time, any place. I don't even have to survive—just me, alone, even dead, would be enough to do the job—and there are a lot of us now, Seiglein. A lot. Talk it over, bring it up to the Nine Families. Consider it. Then, broadcast your response on Band 241—it's not used for much. I'll be monitoring. If you wish to talk, we'll talk. Otherwise—more, Seiglein. More and more and more. Maybe I'll even turn *you* into a Choz. Think about it. I'll be listening—and I'll be in touch."

I signed off. I knew they'd be out to the beacon as soon as they could after getting the message, and I had no intention of being there when they did. I drained the water and atmosphere systems into my reserve tanks, and left it for them, cold, empty, ready to be blown up.

I L-jumped back toward in-system.

We passed several cycles going over the raid, the mistakes we made, our own hopes and fears—and we watched Marsha, still alive but still out, a wreck.

The younger ones could not condemn her—they, too, had felt that tremendous sense of power, the exhilarating sense of being where they belonged.

But by the ninth cycle there was still nothing on Band 241. I began to worry now, to wonder if I had miscalculated. Finally, I could stand it no longer.

"George—let's monitor off St. Cyril," I suggested, and he agreed.

The planet, of course, was externally unchanged from the way it had been before the raid. But, we knew, things were happening down there, strange and terrible to the people that we'd hit.

We could hear their frantic transmissions.

". . . Crazy stuff's all over the place," came one voice. "It grows and spreads faster than you can chop it down. You root it out, kill it with sprays, and you find a patch ten times bigger somewhere else. I don't know what . . ."

And later: ". . . going crazy. Some of them broke into the food stores and ate like they were starving. They've gone crazy—and I feel like I'm starving myself . . ."

And much later still, as Band 241 stayed silent: ". . . lying around in comas just out on the grass or something. A few of them are eating the damned stuff. I feel so damned light-headed, high, I don't know what it is. Some disease . . . Your bio boys better get in and cure this thing, fast!"

Ah! The faith man had in his magical technology and in his leaders!

". . . animals. I had this extreme craving to eat the grass outside today—and I did! I still feel funny, crazy, but some of the others are further along. The docs got it too, so they're no help at all. I barely dragged myself in here to send this. God! My arms are dragging the ground when I'm standing up! You wouldn't believe . . ."

But they *would* believe, I knew. They'd know.

Medical teams came from the southern cities, and tried their best, but, before long, the virus had their measure and they, too, were more interested in sleeping and eating. Once started, the process allowed little time for other things.

And still Band 241 was silent.

What was taking them so long? I wondered. Was Seiglein content to ignore this? Even if he somehow failed to get my message it should be obvious by now what was happening on St. Cyril. Or were they waiting to convince themselves, to see how far it would go on this scale?

Man was his own worst enemy on St. Cyril. Not knowing what was happening and getting no help from their government and corporations, they had taken the victims from some of the construction camps to their city labs and hospitals to study. In hours they had done years of the virus's work. Long ahead of schedule, the virus was loosed on the centers of population on St. Cyril.

Through this time, Marsha clung tenaciously to the thread of life, we gave Shem a Christian burial in space, and Band 241 remained silent.

George played with the virus. He was getting strong signals from St. Cyril, but too many to sort out. My computer was better than Moses, of course, but it wasn't designed for this sort of thing. He finally could narrow down reception to a small area and certain type of virus, but this was just a variation of the way we'd kept contact with Marsha's band.

He played with their acidic secretions, those things

that could break down even a spaceship wall if necessary. He had some success, to judge by the radio reports, but there were too many different things composed in too many different ways; it would take a much larger computer to handle all the stuff.

By the twenty-first cycle of monitoring, the effects were spreading in the cities. The medical men and scientists were the first to be hit, of course—they'd been in direct contact with the virus. The largely defenseless and technologically dependent test colonies started to grind to a halt, and gardens, grass plots, and groves started sprouting this funny grass and these tuber plants.

As power and maintenance systems failed, panic set in. There were riots, terrible bouts of madness, even before the hunger struck the cities. Thousands were killed in these, thousands more in the crazed scramble for food as the thing took hold.

Chaos reigned as the change swept civilization on St. Cyril.

It was a horrible, frightening spectacle.

Since Band 241 stayed empty, I prayed someone was watching. I felt guilty as hell as things went on, although I couldn't quite understand why.

A few cycles later we discovered what they were up to.

The sensors went off and I jumped. Something had just come out of L-jump not far from us!

I checked, saw a large blip, somewhere between the little destroyer class and something the size of the *Courrant*. It was pretty far away, but I knew it was a military-class ship and that it had me as well. I backed off, causing some consternation with the speed of the getaway and lack of warning.

The ship fired at me, but I had the jump on him and was into a quick L-jump before the robomissiles could reach us. Oddly, I was in the only kind of ship that could do that and get away with it—scout ships were built for speed and maneuverability; most of the others couldn't even land.

I pulled out of the jump, not apologizing to anybody, and, to my shock, saw more missiles not very far from me. They had seen my energy deflection on their sensors and changed for me. I still had some velocity from coming out of the jump and managed to make another, but I knew that I was out of there with seconds or less to spare. The bastard had fired a random 360-degree spread at me, guessing I'd make an emergency short jump!

I laid off, coming out only a few minutes later, half-expecting to meet more company.

There wasn't any, but I was still close enough to the system to be able, in a couple of minutes, to receive intense radiation from the vicinity of the space I'd just occupied.

Those missiles had been so close they'd detonated.

The close shave actually helped me, in that the captain, smart as he obviously was, would believe that they'd gotten me—the missiles wouldn't detonate unless their sophisticated computer brains told them they could hurt the target.

My computer's better than your computer, I thought smugly.

George was picking himself up off the wall. They'd all been thrown about quite a bit, and some were groaning, but they'd be all right. Marsha we had webbed down, so she had been the best prepared of all of us even if she didn't know it.

"What the hell was *that* about?" George roared, and there were several angry seconds.

Quickly, I explained what happened, and they calmed down. For a few it suddenly sunk in that we'd almost been zapped.

George looked worried. "Do you suppose they're going to do a Patmos operation on St. Cyril?" he asked, more of himself than me. "That's dumb—we'll just do it again and again. They *must* know that."

"They may think they got us," I pointed out. "And they don't know about the *Nijinsky*. That disappearance is just one of the mysteries of space."

He shook his head. "No, they can't really know that was us back there. I think they just figured we were part of the routine traffic and wanted to be sure we hadn't been down there, maybe a new carrier. No, that's not the plot. They came here to do something, not catch us."

I frowned. "I'm not sure I want to try that captain again," I told him. "He's good—very good."

The biologist nodded. "I agree. No use in letting him know we're alive anyway. We can wait. Any signs as to what he's doing?"

I shook my head. "It'd be several minutes before the energy pulses would reach us here anyway. Don't forget our velocity is geometric. We're a good ways from St. Cyril."

George sat up on his tail and cocked his head, thinking.

"Now, let's see," he mumbled, "what would I do if I were they? Bomb it out? No, not this time. That failed before." He looked at me. "Fix any spacecraft down there or in orbital station that might have been contaminated so they can't go anyplace, that's for sure."

"Right," I agreed. "I'd hate to have to make a planetfall from anywhere in the next few days. I'll bet they'll zap half a dozen innocent ships too slow with the answers."

He shrugged. "Spreading panic is part of our own operation. Remember, fifteen of us are taking on seven hundred billion people. No, we have to think. If they gave in to us, they'd lose. It's surrender, nothing less. We would dictate terms."

"But our terms are pretty mild!" I pointed out. "St. Cyril would be enough!"

"They don't know that," George pointed out. "Besides, it's enough for a while, but that wouldn't last forever. You must know that as much as they. And we're biologically compatible in the most basic respect—we need the same kind of worlds. You yourself told me the odds on finding a new Terraformable world. They'd have to halve that at least—and we can breed faster, Choziform anything compatible with the virus. Their whole economy, their whole system is based upon continued expansion. They'll know that."

"But we've been over this a hundred times before," I protested.

"That was different. Planning a great expedition and getting the result you expect are two different things. Plotters have stars in their eyes—we had to. We had no choice but to do this."

"So they aren't blowing the place up—not yet, anyway," I summed up. "I'd have gotten the energy pulses by now. And they aren't giving in to us, either. So what *are* they doing?"

"If I were they, I'd buy time—as much time as possible," the biologist replied. "First, I'd quarantine St. Cyril, so I'd have some samples of what I was up against. Seiglein blew it with Patmos—he let Moses get away, he missed us, and then he blew up the only place that would give him the clues to meet a future threat. He was dumb. The Nine Families aren't dumb as a group. No, I'd keep St. Cyril and let it be Choziformed—and I'd watch, and keep notes, and I'd study it."

"But they can't get too close," I pointed out. "The virus will get them, too."

George shrugged. "They can drop nurds and analyze the stuff in chambers like you have, only better, with the best computers and best biological minds they have. It'll be tough, but eventually they'll come up with something."

"Like what?" I asked, getting a little nervous now. The others were crowded around, listening as well.

The Web of the Chozen

"An antitoxin, something that would kill the virus but nothing else."

I thought about that one. "That's possible?"

He nodded. "Oh, certainly. There's a cure for everything sooner or later. Kill the virus and you destroy the Choz, but leave the place Terraformable. That's what St. Cyril will be—their lab. The people down there will be their lab animals. Sooner or later they'll find the answer."

I felt crushed. I looked over at Marsha, still unconscious. I thought of Shem, floating somewhere out there, forever.

For nothing.

All for nothing.

One of the younger members of the raiding party looked stricken, and said what we all were thinking then.

"Then, we've lost," he said in anguish.

I looked at him, at George, at Marsha, at the ship. I thought about the colony on the *Nijinsky,* the billions dead on Patmos. I thought about being shot at, tricked, suckered, pushed around by everybody from the Seiglein Corporation to Moses to circumstance.

It boiled up in me, in a fury that must have shown a frightening, dangerous aura to the others. They edged away from me.

It wasn't going to end like this. It. Was. Not. Going. To. End. Like. This!

I whirled around, shouting for Cain to take his perch above the control board.

"*Nobody* beats Bar Holliday!" I said with grim menace. I turned to them, my aura so bright I could almost feel it. "Prepare for L-jump," I snapped. The alarm rang, the figures were in.

"Where are we going?" George asked nervously.

"Back," I said, not looking around. "Back to the *Nijinsky.* Back to take one last, desperate gamble."

Nineteen

We took only a few minutes to transfer Marsha and clear out my scout, then I sent for Ham.

He was bursting to hear the details of the raid, but I dismissed his questions curtly. If time was what Seiglein and the others wanted, then time was something they'd not get a second more of than I could manage. My manner and hue told him this was no time to balk.

"Look, Ham, I really need Marsha on this, but without her you'll have to do. She taught you everything she'd ever known about the *Nijinsky*."

He nodded. "I know every bolt in the bucket. You know that."

"I'm counting on you!" I responded emphatically. "Look, I want to get into the modular section of the *Nijinsky* computer. Can you get me and Cain there?"

He looked nervous and dubious. "C'mon, Bar! You can't fool with that stuff. One slip and you could kill us!"

"But you know where it is and how the net is set up," I persisted.

He resisted, but he *did* know, and as much as he would have fought anyone else, he could not fight me.

We went to the stern, and beyond, into a tiny room with an elevator platform.

"We only go down every once in a while to check," he said nervously. "Rough ride."

I made sure Cain was scrunched in with us, and

Ham punched the control square with his nose. We descended.

We stopped at the lowest level, in the service bay of the freighter. There was a great deal of vibration here from the generators, pumps, recirculating equipment, and the like that kept us going and would for the next fifty years or more at current levels.

We made our way laboriously down a passageway not meant for Choz, a long, long way to the point just under the ship's midsection. A large metal plate blocked our path.

"There's another access from the bow," Ham remarked, "and it ends about a hundred and fifty meters from here in another metal plate. That's the core, Bar. It's behind there."

I scanned the wall. It looked extremely solid, but I knew it had to be removable in some way. I fine-scanned the whole thing, line by line, square centimeter by square centimeter.

And there they were—special bolts with odd shape and size, set flush and disguised as part of the metal superstructure so that a sighted person would never have known they were there.

I turned to Cain. "Odd bolts," I told the robot. "Look, I'll touch one. They're in a pattern from that point. See them?"

The robot scampered up to the wall, then climbed supporting itself half on the wall and half on the panel. It took a free tentacle and felt the bolts, each of the nine in turn.

"Can you get them out?" I asked him, nervous myself now.

It prodded one lightly. "I believe so," it replied in its electronic monotone. "However, there are charges in each bolt. If not removed in a certain order they will fuse."

I sighed. "Any clue as to the order?"

"None," it replied. "It will have to be tried randomly."

"That's it, then," Ham said, almost cheerily. "You can't get in."

I wasn't put off so easily.

"Cain, if they're programmed for a certain order, then they're linked to the brain in some way?"

"I do not believe so," it replied. "There is some connector there. I believe the determination is mechanical."

I brightened. "You mean it's a series of gears or levers?"

"Yes," it replied. "I can feel it."

I thought for a moment. What could show the linkages to Cain without lousing up everything?

"Couldn't we cut through?" I suggested.

"We might," the robot admitted. "But it is a question of whether we would also injure the computer. I cannot do anything that would injure the computer. That is a mandated pattern in my programming."

"Uh huh," was all I could say. I thought carefully. "How thick is it? Any idea?"

"Not very," Cain responded. "I cannot determine for certain, but I would say it would not be more than three hundred and ninety nor less than three hundred and seventy millimeters."

"Close enough," I said drily. "Cain, how can you feel the couplers?"

"Through the engine vibration," the robot responded. "The mechanism is flush with the plate, and vibrates slightly against it."

"Then," I suggested hopefully, "suppose we could vibrate it constantly, at a much higher sound level, same frequency."

"That might work," Cain responded.

"Ham," I said sharply. "Go get George."

Just as we could broadcast through the virus on the ground at St. Cyril, George could do the same for Ham and me from the scout to the *Nijinsky* hold. We drafted others, and formed a living message chain all the way back to George.

Without me on the scout, he had no way of knowing what was going on.

"Tell George to go ahead," I said to the man behind me, and so on down the incredibly long line it went. All of us nearest the plate faced it; I used all males, because our larger horns and rounder membranes produced more intense sound.

The tone started, and I found it strange; I went blind, because it was outside my own reception limit, down in the bass, really, but I was also out of control —I couldn't *not* broadcast.

"Cain!" I called out. "Got it?"

"More intensity," came the response, almost masked in the tonal din.

"Tell George maximum intensity, and give it to everybody down here!" I called back, and so it went. About three minutes later I got what I asked for.

I don't know how long it was; probably not long, but it seemed like forever. Suddenly I heard Cain, hanging from the ceiling over me. The robot couldn't be heard otherwise.

"I have it now," he said, and I could have kissed his spidery, mechanical hide.

It took longer to turn us off; the sound was so intense that I had a hell of a time being heard, and Cain finally had to make its way up to get the message across.

From this point, the job was simple. We'd apply a little webbing to the tip of one of Cain's tentacles, and he'd slap it immediately on the bolt. It would harden, bonding the two, and the bolt would turn. Then we'd have to free him by tossing small bowls of urine held in our mouths—not exactly pleasant, I can assure you—and do it again.

Finally, the plate loosened, creaked, and fell down with a crash, almost nipping my legs in the process.

I went into the computer core, scanning it carefully. Finally I found what I was looking for—a storage rack, with hundreds of tiny round programming modules.

I really needed Marsha, but I would have to do it alone, I knew.

"Cain!" I called. The robot scampered in and waited, expectant. "Can you put these little balls in that chute over there, in the order they are laid out, top to bottom?"

"The seventh one in the ninth row is missing," it pointed out.

"I know. Can't be helped. It's already in there. Okay, can you do it?"

"Easily," responded the robot, and did just that.

I burned. I burned with hatred, I burned with the fires of passion and desperation.

"What are they, Bar?" Ham asked, scared to death at the exposure of his precious computer.

"One hundred and four little programming course balls," I replied. "One for each possible destination of the *Nijinsky*. Now we'll go to the bridge and get a course readout for each."

"What are you gonna do, anyway?" he asked me, confused.

They were all there, all the ward leaders who would take the word back to the people. Nothing stayed quiet in a society this small, but I wanted it done right.

George was there, too. He already knew what I was planning, and could say nothing more.

"All right, people," I began hesitantly. "This is our situation, so listen good. Right now there's a human ship analyzing the world we hit, trying to find a way to kill the virus. Kill it and you kill us. You've already heard that. This puts us in a bind." I paused for effect, then continued.

The Web of the Chozen

"First, we can jump for the unknown stars. I can stay out and make about three hundred jumps. The *Nijinsky* could make maybe twenty. The odds of us finding a planet of our own in that range would be slim, and we'd be out there, waiting for the systems to finally give out, if we didn't."

"So we're dead," said one older leader, I think it was Beth, one of Marsha's second breed, not mine.

"We have one chance," I told them. "One chance only. There are over thirteen hundred of us. There are one hundred and four human worlds. Allowing some leeway, for ship's maintenance and the like, that's twelve of us for every human world."

"You mean—land on *all* of them?" gasped one named Ruth.

"I mean exactly that," I responded. "And now— before they get a key to the virus and before they get smart enough to think of it themselves and really defend against it."

"But—how long would this take?" another asked.

"About two years," I responded. "But, remember, it takes just as much time for *them* to move as it does for us—and they can't build their defenses fast enough. If you're good, and if we have a little luck, many of you won't be discovered until it's far too late."

"They'll kill us," one breathed.

"Many of us," I admitted. "Perhaps most of us. I hope not. But—there it is. If anybody else has a plan, let me know. Otherwise, we do it."

"There should be a vote!" Ruth protested. "We can't ask the people to do this without a vote!"

"Extermination or the survival of the race," George broke in. "That's what it is, all right. Which one do *you* vote for?"

"My God!" one swore. "To—to turn every human into the Choz! It's incredible!"

I smiled. "Yes, isn't it?" I agreed, a trace of malice in my voice. "So much so they'll never figure out what

205

we're doing until it's too late. Then *let* them come up with a way to kill the virus without killing themselves!"

They left, left to tell the others, to make preparations, to get themselves mentally ready for the task.

George and I weren't alone—no Choz was ever really alone, not until we broke out of these ships—but it was as much privacy as any ever had.

I was grinning, thinking of the Seigleins and the Huangs and the Smombas and the others of the Nine Families as they changed into Choz.

Oh, I'd have my revenge, all right! On all of them!

I looked at George, and saw that he was grinning, too.

"So we all might win," he said lightly.

"What the hell do you mean?" I responded, knowing I was missing something.

"The revolution!" he laughed. "And what a revolution! No more humanity! No more tight little niches full of Creatovision addicts and stagnancy! The constant pressure for new worlds, for expansion!"

"Those vegetables in the superquads won't change anything except their routine," I pointed out. "You yourself said that Patmos was a nice analog of human society."

"You saw what happened on St. Cyril," he replied. "Panic, riots, a terrible thing. The Change itself will weed out the least fit. The rest—well, their spark might come out. And we still have the technology —the computers, the bulk of man's knowledge and experience. It's a new start!"

"We may wind up a herd of cows after all," I countered darkly.

He shrugged. "Starts are starts. Man was at an end. Now we start him again. I leave it to generations unborn to do it again differently. In two years, maybe less man will know he's a dinosaur. In three, that's what he'll be. And man will be the Chosen, starting new."

"We could get shot out of the sky on the second try," I noted.

He shook his head. "Oh, no. We've come too far, done too much. This is what had to happen, Bar! Nobody would have accepted it until now, but I knew. I've always known. We'll *win*, Bar! We were destined to win! That's why all this has happened. God works in mysterious ways, His wonders to perform!"

Twenty

And, of course, you know he was right. I still haven't been able to accept George's ideas of God and destiny but we seeded almost half the human worlds before anybody really caught on; we hit all hundred and four before we were through.

The ships and personnel that took off and landed helped us, carried the virus faster than we could.

They finally *did* surrender when they realized just how extensive the seeding was. They'd killed a lot of us. But of the original twelve hundred, some four hundred and eighty survived.

A much better percentage than that of humanity when it Changed.

But, that's all right, too. George knew more about the virus than anybody, and when the top scientists of humanity themselves were Choz, they took his brilliant work and amplified it.

The social system's still in flux, of course. Not everyone is a revolutionary or a world-beater. Still, it's a new age, and, as George predicted, it was a new beginning.

And there *were* robots, and there *were* computers, to help design new devices, new ways of adapting things of technology, factories, and salve jars, to Choz form and requirements.

So here we are, a race of near-immortals, a race more in control of its body and its destiny than any one human ever could have been.

Oh, there are still *some* humans about. Some of

them in ships, stations, and the like who held out as we held out, but who could not hold out forever. We've managed almost total control of the virus now; the few thousand remaining humans were protected from it, and a small colony remains, a curiosity in the backwaters of history.

The corporations collapsed, of course. A Choz is totally self-sufficient if it has an adequate food supply.

In a way, Moses' plans for humanity were carried out, although I'm sure not to the result he intended.

We often think of that as we're out in the unknown sectors, looking for new worlds to conquer, looking for a new race with a different culture, an alien race that is no longer as frightening as it was. It's out there —the odds say it is.

Moses is out there, too, of course, and he did have organic material to work with. We worry about that a lot; there might well be another race of proto-Choz out there, one not to our liking. We're ready for it, I think. Ready and waiting.

I say "we" of course. Oh, I could have been the leader of this new order, but that's more in George's line. I'm just happy that many of my children, including Eve, are so prominent in building the new society.

As for me—well, things are rather too hectic, too confused in a program so total, so complete.

I like being out with the stars, out finding new worlds, making those first discoveries.

And I'm not alone. Marsha pulled through, incredibly, by willpower alone. Pulled through and waited, a helpless cripple, the three agonizing years until the new Choz science could produce a massive regeneration.

So there it is—the oral record everybody's wanted of what happened from the great Bar Holliday's point of view. Do with it what you will, judge me as you will; I'll be out among my stars, looking for what nobody's seen before.

The Web of the Chozen

With the stars, a good ship, and Marsha, I have what *I* want. You go find your own place in the scheme of things. Just remember:

Nobody beats Bar Holliday.

ABOUT THE AUTHOR

JACK L. CHALKER was born in Norfolk, Virginia, on December 17, 1944, but was raised and has spent most of his life in Baltimore, Maryland. He learned to read almost from the moment of entering school, and by working odd jobs had amassed a large book collection by the time he was in junior high school, a collection now too large for containment in his present quarters. Science fiction, history, and geography all fascinated him early on, interests which continue.

Chalker joined the Washington Science Fiction Association in 1958 and began publishing an amateur SF journal, *Mirage*, in 1960. After high school he decided to be a trial lawyer, but money problems and the lack of a firm caused him to switch to teaching. He holds B.S. degrees in history and English, and an M.L.A. from the Johns Hopkins University. He has been teaching history and geography in the Baltimore public schools since 1966. Additionally, out of the amateur journals he founded a publishing house, The Mirage Press, Ltd., devoted to nonfiction and bibliographic works on science fiction and fantasy. This company has produced more than twenty books in the last eight years. His hobbies include working on science-fiction convention committees, guest lecturing on SF to institutions like the Smithsonian, esoteric audio, and travel. He is an active conservationist and

National Parks supporter, and he has an intensive love for ferryboats, with the avowed goal of riding every ferry in the world. He is single, and still lives and works in Baltimore.